A SCORE OF STORIES

M D CURD

ISBN NO.9798863970783

Copyright@ M D Curd 2023
The moral rights of the author have been asserted.

All characters in this publication are fictitious and any resemblance to real persons, living or dead, is purely coincidental.

All Rights reserved.

No part of this publication may be reproduced, stored in a retrieval system or transmitted, in any form or by any means, without the prior permission in writing of the author, nor be otherwise circulated in any form of binding or cover other than that in which it is published and without a similar condition including this condition being imposed on the subsequent purchaser.

Dedicated to my husband Tony

CONTENTS

WHEN THE WIND BLOWS

REMEMBERING HAREBELLS

PERSUASION OF THE GODS

A NEW MILLENNIUM?

THE GOAT'S SHOEHORN

A PLAY ON WORDS

A DROP TOO MUCH

AN AFFLICTION OF THE EYE

CHAIN OF EVENTS

DAMASK ROSES

NIGHT DRINKERS

THE DINNER LADY

THE FISHING BOAT

UNWELCOME ENCOUNTERS

THE ATTIC

THE BIG THREE O

HAVE ANOTHER BEER

UNNATURAL CAUSES

FLEETING SHADES

INTO THE LIGHT

FLASH FICTION:-

A STAB IN THE DARK

BIRD TALK

I COULD HAVE LAUGHED....

KARMA CHAMELEON

TELL THE BEES

THE DROP

A ZOO INMATE ADDRESSES HIS VISITORS

WHEN THE WIND BLOWS

Mark felt the full strike of the strobe light against his eyes before he saw the 'shadow flicker'. He dived towards the kitchen floor. As his damp hands slipped along the tiles, he prevented a direct collision with his forehead. He dragged his leaden body to the legs of the nearest chair, propped himself against it, and waited for the closing in of his vision. *Too late now, anyway*; he thought.

It was dusk when he opened his eyes again. He rubbed away the stickiness in his tear ducts and swallowed back the metallic taste in his mouth. Struggling upright, he crossed the room to drag the curtains closed to cover the window.

Unable to avert his gaze, he had to pause and look out of the window. A glimpse turned into a prolonged stare, although the dizzyingly tall, white tower repelled him to the point of nausea. His eyes travelled up the length of it; from foundation, to the top of the white column, and the business part of it. He heard the blades rip through the air – Whoosh! Whoosh! Then the whine of the generator – a slewing, mechanical, grating sound. Could he really hear it? Even inside this room, with the windows closed?

Mark sipped the last dregs of a mug of hot tea and laced up his walking boots. The drab day had begun with drizzling rain. He unlatched his front door and headed for the little copse he loved, which opened out at an angle beyond the short distance of his back garden. He looked back at his house, nestling, solitary, in the hamlet's dip.

His boots shuffled against the leaves in a comforting, soft crackle, and he savoured the acrid smell of the earth and the fallen foliage. The year was turning, and he thought that the muted light dissolving downwards through the canopy heralded the death of the summer sunshine which had so troubled him.

Out of habit, he crossed from the outskirts of the copse to the public footpath and bridleway. Because he knew where he was going, his heart beat in an unsteady rhythm, the harbinger of palpitations, as he neared his objective. A gradual awareness came to him that the thud of his heart echoed the heavy tread of a horse behind him. The animal was being restrained to less than a trot.

She saw him first, reined in, and drew to a halt. "Good morning, Mark. How are you?"

Mark moved closer to the horse and stroked his neck so that the horse nuzzled against him. "Wish I had something for you, Jumper. Sorry, nothing in my pockets," he said.

He stepped back to look up at the rider, for courtesy's sake, and mumbled, "Oh, not too bad, Joan. How was the harvest?" His face felt stiff in the attempt to smile.

"Fair to middling. You should have come to the harvest supper. Almost the entire village was there. You always *used* to come. You've not been well?" She straightened the horse with a tender tug on the bridle. "I heard something in the village ... Poor you, still getting the headaches?"

Mark nodded, stepped further back into the hedge, and gestured for her to pass him. He watched horse and rider moving along the path, picking up pace, and saw her turn to wave back at him.

When he reached the familiar gap in the hedge – a broken down, whitish gap of twisted hazel – he felt for the binoculars in his pocket. He stood looking up, studying the sky as if he was training his sight on a bird of prey, or even the trailing flight of a distant aeroplane. The village lay beneath a flight path. Someone could see him as doing just that, he thought. But it was all a mental subterfuge.

Close up and enlarged in its grotesqueness, his focus re-aligned on the wind turbine. His heart raced. Yet he had to look.

Is that a crack? At the base. Is that a hairline crack? Now the blades. The mottling on their surface – signs of disintegration of the fabric, whatever they made it of? It's faulty, dangerous, the whole terrible structure!

*****

That evening, he visited the village pub. He strolled for ten minutes down the hill. John, the pub landlord, had lit the first log fire of the season, and the blast of warm air hit him as he entered. There were only a few men clustered around the bar, perched on stools.

"Evening, Mark. Long time, no see. How are you doing?"

In the end, he bought a round and managed a couple of pints himself. The conversation revolved around the harvest, the weather, the way milk prices were dropping. They asked about his business; whether he got enough commissions and how the sales of his wood carvings were going.

When he left, Mark knew they would talk about him for a bit. He imagined the talk edging back to all the earlier arguments, all the upset he had caused when the project started. Of course, the farmer had wanted *his* pay-off for having the wind turbine on his land, and the villagers wanted the new roof for the community hall: *their* pay-off. None of them had a house anywhere near as close to the damn thing as he did.

Wind's getting up; he thought, as he trailed his way back up the hill by the light of the large rubber-handled torch he always carried. Stopping on the outskirts of the copse, he stood listening to the creaking of the trees. He imagined the swaying of the individual trees, within the vague outline, which was all he could see. There would be more leaf-fall by the morning.

Of course, they had no time for his concerns. Nobody believed him about the effects produced by the low light of the sun behind the turbine's blades. Nobody could imagine how his house filled with the strobe lights, whether he was looking out of the window (which they had all advised him *not to do*), or whether he was facing away from it. Sometimes it caught him even when he was in the rear of his house, huddled away at the back of his workshop.

How could he prove it? The strobe sensation lasted for ten, maybe twelve seconds, and others could not predict or witness the phenomenon. After the noisy, prolonged five months of the installation, the village had ignored all his attempts to show them the reports. They were uninterested by the investigations into 'shadow flicker'. It sounded incongruous, didn't it? Lame, perhaps, he sometimes thought.

'Mark, poor chap, he suffers from migraines,' they said. He had heard them.

That night, he took a double dose of his pills to make sure he slept. The wind was roaring but, through all the noise, he could not pick out the whine of the generator at the top of the tower behind the rotor blades. The wind speeds must be pretty high, he reckoned, and the automatic brake must have stopped them turning. He tweaked at the curtain in his bedroom. It revealed a sky in turmoil under churning moon-lit clouds. Rain sheeted down the glass like a shiny, plastic waterfall. There was majesty in it.

Mark suddenly felt a need to speak to someone, just to hear another voice. He switched on his mobile and touched the screen against her number. *Nothing. No signal. Must be the storm.*

Sleep soon came after the heavy combination of alcohol and his medication. He thought he dreamt of ripping and tearing in rage at his own bed linen, but in reality it was the noise outside impinging through to his consciousness as he opened wide his eyes.

At first, he was aware only of the bed vibrating, of his body slipping, inching from side to side across it. In a flash of lightning through the torn curtain, he saw the shards of myriad shattered glass. They were from his bedroom window. Half-awake, he registered beauty in the colours.

Almost soothed, he gasped in rigid horror as he watched

the ceiling belly downwards. The explosive rip of the roof galvanised him to roll and fling himself out of the bed, dragging the duvet with him. In a blast of cold air, he breathed in powdery dust and spluttered and coughed. Strips of debris menaced him now; jagged metal and splintered wood hanging down. A trickle channelled across his forehead. All sound was now muffled, and he realised that something must have happened to his ears. In a final shudder of disbelief, he watched the breach in the roof widen and fill with a heavy, blinding white.

*****

"It's me, Mark. Elizabeth. Your wife. You poor love!" Mark turned his head with great care and waited for a stab of pain, but none came this time. He registered that the hospital bed was hard and the linen drawn across his body too tight for comfort. It was quiet, though, and at least he was alive.

She was too close to him, leaning over him. He could not focus on her face, only the flashy ring on one finger of her hand as she brushed it against his hair and tried to say something, but it was too difficult. No comprehensible sound had erupted from his mouth because she retreated; he heard the backward scrape of a chair. *I must be in a bad way if she's come.*

He tried to remember how long it was since they had parted company for good. Time here seemed to have elongated; it felt nebulous and determined by the hospital routine of meals and the changing of the dressings. It had to be more than a year since he had seen her at her new house in the town. 'A trial separation', Elizabeth had called it. But she indefinitely extended the trial quarter by quarter, and it never reached a verdict.

She was the first visitor that he knew of. The first since he had awoken, almost fully conscious in the hospital, anyway. It could only have been a matter of days. He winced as an image flashed across his vision. *My house, my refuge! Is it destroyed? Will I ever be able to return?* Perhaps she had seen his tears because she was back now, bending over him and stroking his cheek. He felt sick and swallowed back bile. *Nothing could survive that. Not even the strongest of constructions – and my house was never that!* He tried again to mouth a question. He wanted to know how much damage that infernal structure had done to his home.

"Tower?" She repeated the word, as a question, and close to his ear. Then silence slid between them again. Mark flung his arms out wide, agitated, showing her he had to know. He rocked his body, tried to turn on his side. Perhaps she would think he was trying to get out of the bed? He heard raised voices.

The pin prick of the injection soothed him. Within a minute, the calming sensation had followed.

Elizabeth was leaning over him again. "The tower. I understand now. You thought it was the *wind turbine*? But it's still there, Mark. Concrete and steel it's made of – you know that," she said.

The image came to him again of the hideous, looming, enormous whiteness blocking the night sky through his open roof on that stormy night. *What does she mean? Of course it was that.*

"It was a tree, Mark! That's what shattered your roof. One tree from your beloved copse caused all the damage!"

He drifted away then, not wanting to know any more.

REMEMBERING HAREBELLS

This is what I remember. I hear the unlatching of the door and Kate comes in just as I'm carving a thick slice of bread from the loaf on the table. The first thing I notice is her bare feet. Well, that's not unusual for this place, and it is a better time of year now than some other holidays up here on the moors.

'Guess how far I've been, Heather! It's a wonderful, wonderful morning, and I was up and out with the dawn. And look, I've picked these – harebells, they are,' she says all in one breath. She rushes forward over the cold flags, her bunch of blue flowers scattered in their fall onto the table, as she wraps her arms around my neck and shoulders, squeezing tightly and laughing all the while.

'Sit down and eat something; this is more of a brunch than breakfast,' I say, even though she nearly chokes me before she settles on the wooden bench and grabs my piece of bread.

There is bacon ready grilled in the oven and eggs, which I fry. I made coffee, too, on the range. A slow process, everything so rustic here in the stone cottage, but we are used to it now. I can make a basic stew, which lasts us for days. Kate is hopeless. She just forgets everything and spends all her time outdoors. When we first came, we used the inns of the smaller villages to get a hot meal. We seldom bother with any of that now.

Her cheeks are blush red and her eyes bright and full of mischief as she pulls at my arm to tip more coffee into her cup. She gives me a pinch and giggles at my expression of mock horror. 'Pinch, punch, first of the month,' she says. I had forgotten the date. Her brown locks look wild and frizzed. By the wind, of course, even though she says static causes it. What static, out here in the wilderness? Strange how her beautiful hair returns to the neat, straight frame and pelmet fringe as soon as we return home to the city down south.

Walking, that is Kate's particular joy. More like running; up and down the hillsides, goat-like, gulping in the air as she stands on huge jutting boulders with her hair flaring out behind her, swept up by the wind. She sings too. Nonsense, I call it, but she says it is old folk songs in dialect. She researches everything, and what she has not studied she seems to have as innate knowledge.

She gets up, her mouth still crammed with food, to look at my picture.

Painting that is my way of relaxing, although huddled on the moors in the perpetual blasts, or dashing back drenched by sudden cloudbursts is not so rewarding. I take photos, too, and can work from those in the weather's worst.

She fingers my clean palette knife resting on the ledge of the easel. Kate likes to see how thickly I apply the streaks of paint and now she holds the knife aloft like some kind of Amazonian – except she is nothing like such a mythological figure; she is petite, fragile even, unlike me. She strikes a pose.

There is a pretty good skyscape on the canvas Kate is now looking at, stooping low by the makeshift easel to peer close up.

'I know that place!' she says.

I get up to join her in front of the easel 'What do you mean? It's only a few ruined bits of wall I found a few days ago, which I took a photo of. I have elaborated on it, made more of the structure than is actually there, Kate. You *can't* recognise that.' I gesture at the romanticised building I have created.

'Take me to it, Heather.' She untangles her legs from around the bench and is by the door, beckoning me on, before I have even taken a breath. Kate is manic today, and I look towards the dresser where her pills were. She catches my glance, grabs me by the hand, and drags me outside.

She is right. It is still a sparkling day, with a few clouds overhead, none of which are rushing by at great speed. The place is at a fair distance, in a small dell, as I remember and after a while I run ahead, leading her on, catching her excitement. She whoops and swirls like a bird most of the way, back-tracking and leaping forward again. When I finally see the place, I wait for her so that we can climb down into the dip together. We see the low, broken walls beneath us. Bracken guards the perimeter of what once must have been a small cottage. I see blood welling up from a scratch on her leg. 'Don't go any further, Kate, you're bleeding.'

But she is insistent, so I sweep her up, laughing, and carry her across what must have been the threshold of the entrance, marked by two worn, pitted stones, puddled with water and slimy with blackened moss. When I put Kate down, she says, 'I love you, Heather. Heart and soul. We could even get married now, couldn't we?' I smile and kiss her before she can twist away, embarrassed by her boldness and certainty.

She paces along what she perceives as the outline of the building, solitary and thoughtful, her shoulders hunched, and wraps her arms around herself as if she is feeling cold. The dell seems damp, dark. Not as I had painted it.

Kate struggles up a bank to the north side of the ruins, clutching at convenient tufts of vegetation, and stops to look down at me from the heights. 'Did you call me? What name did you call me? Not Kate,' she shouts. 'Nor Catherine. Did you call me Cathy?'

Bemused, I don't reply, but after a while we leave and wander back together in silence, arm in arm. She lifts her head now and then, turns and listens. 'It's an owl.' I say. 'You told me they are active at dusk.'

That evening, Kate is excitable again and wants to take me to another special place she has found. She insists we must go this night, after our frugal supper of leftovers. There is nearly a full moon and here, where light pollution is negligible, she says the sky will be peppered with stars, and I can name all the constellations for her. It is a game we have played before. Another game. Like the way she sometimes calls me by my surname, Clifford.

I take a powerful torch and insist she is properly shod. At the last moment, I drape one of my thick jackets over her shoulders.

We climb down from a vertiginous escarpment, and she takes the torch to throw the beam onto a long mound of rough grass, strangely levelled off. 'There it is,' Kate says. Moths flutter in the diffused stream of light. She thrusts the torch back into my hands and completes the descent in a few leaps. Standing in front of the mound, with her hands on her hips, I assume this is just a pause in the game.

Kate insists I stretch out on top of the tussocks of grass, which form the shape of the mound. She positions me with care, moving my legs and feet, so that the result is similar to a full penitent before the altar on the floor of a church. She forces my face down. 'Can you breathe?' I mutter agreement. 'Count to twenty. Then be sure to come and find me!' She pats me on the shoulder. I peep and see her throw back her head in laughter and note the direction she takes. She will not go far because even in this moonlight, the going is too difficult. And I have the torch to find her. This is what I remember.

*****

Mrs. Dennis breaks the silence and raises the cup of tea to her lips. Elbows placed firmly on the table which she has assiduously scrubbed, she gives me a hard look. 'Why do you keep coming back, Heather? After all these years, why don't you just sell this place?'

'You forget what people look like. Photos become unreal and I cannot *see* Kate properly any more. But she loved these moors. That's why I come back. Sometimes, it is even harder to bear, you know, when I cannot picture her.'

Mrs. Dennis looks at the new range, nods at the fitted cupboards and all the other improvements in the kitchen. 'You would get a good price. Not as a holiday place, but a proper home for a local young couple, of whatever gender,' she suggests. She turns away and frowns at the sound of rain drumming against the window.

'Make sure *you* don't go wandering tonight,' she says. 'We are in for a storm.'

I ignore her because I know how much Kate loved the sheer wildness of the elements here. I have my own plans for tonight.

The closing sentence of Wuthering Heights

"I lingered round them, under that benign sky: watched the moths fluttering among the heath and harebells, listened to the soft wind breathing through the grass, and wondered how anyone could ever imagine unquiet slumbers for the sleepers in that quiet earth." By Emily Bronte.

PERSUASION OF THE GODS

"I always said that no good decision ever came out of a committee." David shook his fist at his brother, Jonathan. He glared at the others. All six of them peered through the clouds below at the trillions of frogs, legs extended like parachutes, tumbling down. Some had already made splat landings.

"We said at the time, brother, if you remember, that we only intended the suggestion as a trial run. We do not need to justify it yet," Jonathan said. He ran a finger along the edge of an arrow, testing its sharpness. They were not brothers, but it mattered not because they quarrelled like siblings, anyway.

"Well, it will not be the end of the world, will it?" Ruth's busy hands plaited a few corn stalks into the shape of a doll, as her soothing voice urged calm. She knew how to make them compromise without too much difficulty. When you have gleaned a field in a foreign land to stay alive, these matters appeared simpler than they realised. "Committee work always enrages David. It comes from being a king all the time. An important one, we all acknowledge."

"It would surprise you how much the women swayed me." David was musing; he had sat back and fallen into a reverie. "I remember one in particular. I first saw her taking a bath …."

"Yes, I'm sure we can all imagine that," Ruth

interrupted. Her tone was sharp, but she avoided referring to what had followed that obsession; David's part in sending Bathsheba's husband, Uriah, to his death. The times were different, she accepted, and David had indeed produced that long line of leaders, as predicted. The corn doll slipped from her fingers, and she picked it up and caressed it in a moment of abstraction. "As a woman, I was quite capable myself of taking the initiative at times." She added, blushing. Elijah rapped the table and blustered. Spittle shot across the stone table and onto his neighbour. "*Not* the end of the world, Ruth? But that's the whole point! A foretaste, a direct warning to them at least!" His agitated movement and strident tones reduced the two ravens perched on his shoulder to silent pecking, but they dug in their talons to keep their balance and that made him wince.

"It took ten of them last time – the plagues – and even that was not an entirely successful outcome. Neither was the aim the same," said Esther. She continued to adjust her heavy crown. It made her head itch and was as much a penance as a tribute, but it conferred status and you needed to be strong. "There is little subtlety in this measure of the frogs. One needs to be more manipulative, I'm afraid, if we are to persuade the populace.

Mordecai nodded in approval and it was this, with the undoubted truth of Esther's earlier comment, which made them all sit back, breathe deeply and try to summon some inner peace.

"We could send a few thunderbolts," said John. "As to the other nine … I *think* of the locusts with some affection. I lived on them once … with the honey, of course. Good sustenance. And they may well eat insects soon."

Elijah had warned that they were far too modern and augured a descent down a slippery moral slope, but the meditation methods they had adopted seemed to be effective and they now put them into practice almost as an established routine.

Esther had countered Elijah's protests. 'Rubbish!' She had condemned his fury in the one word. 'These practices pre-dated the historical written record of humanity by five or six centuries. I have that on *excellent* authority,' she had added meaningfully.

Now Esther stood up. First, she gestured upwards, then lowered her outstretched arms to shoulder level in a smooth, controlled movement. She began the first 'Om' of the chant.

They all rose to their feet. Some showed more reluctance than others, and joined in the mantra.

*****

Some indefinite centuries later, the committee reported back. Esther expressed the uncountable lapse in time, with admirable logic. "Because we are, in essence, talking about an eternity in which we are fortunate enough to dwell, the precise fixing of any planetary interval with the earth is a … waste of time."

"In that case, I must insist that no-one takes any minutes for this meeting," said David. "As we can't even decide what the date is!"

"How did the frogs go?" asked Jonathan. He tried a distraction in an effort to change the course of the discussion. "Anyone notice a positive outcome?"

"Most of them got eaten," said John. "Especially the legs, by people in some parts of the earth … Gauls, on that land mass, continent …? They saw them as a welcome bounty, rather than to warn them of a forthcoming catastrophe."

"They have endured the other nine plagues in some form or another, on multiple occasions," said Mordecai. "Plenty of wars to pollute the rivers with blood. Disease – both of themselves and other creatures – thunderstorms, fire, hail; all kinds of weather phenomena, and other 'natural disasters', as they call it."

"Some new ones, too. Acid rain, for example," said Ruth.

"Tsunami. Melting of the ice floes. Vast heaving seas, as their levels change, crushing all beneath them and flooding entire land masses. The mere parting of the Red Sea is as nothing in comparison!" said Elijah. He had warmed to the catalogue of disaster, but the committee deemed that as natural for such a tremendous prophet.

"We have failed," said David. "I have to inform you that none of the other groups have come up with anything acceptable, either. It's back to square one now, I think."

"Yes, back to the origins. What has been made, can be unmade, after all," said John.

"No! Wait a moment," said Jonathan. "You realise you are suggesting the end of the world?" He took the sword he was holding and rubbed the tip across his chin. They listened to the rasping. It was a habit of desperation.

"What about the darkness?" Seeing their blank expressions, he elaborated. "The ninth one. But not like an eclipse – they are used to that. They need darkness for a significant period. The prolonged and total absence of the sun. That would have a significant impact, wouldn't it …?"

"A damage limitation exercise," said David. "If we have to go back to the Beginning, at least we can say we tried everything. It doesn't sound so incompetent, does it?"

"Worth a try," said Esther. "They simply won't look after the earth."

The first surprising aspect of the eclipse (in Britain and the western world), was the lack of warning. It was a complete, unexpected phenomenon. It was not mentioned in the media. There was not a glimpse of an excited astronomer. No entrepreneurs produced hand-held frames, with dark cellophane strips, for people to protect their eyes whilst gazing upon it. There were no gatherings of enthusiasts in towns or villages to watch it arrive and, hopefully, pass. No schoolchildren endured preparatory projects to write up and draw images in various mediums.

The second, *frightening* phase, was the inadequacy of energy supplies throughout the world, from pole to desert, and the subsequent bitter cold. The sudden lack of sunlight...

The third and terrifying phenomenon throughout the earth was the death of plants – especially those which had produced food.

QUOTE-"*So Moses stretched out his hand toward the sky, and total darkness covered all Egypt for three days.*" *(Exodus 10 v 21-23)*

A NEW MILLENNIUM?

"What have you got there, John?" Startled, he turned toward the open garage door, rain dripping from it into a gulley after the last of the relentless showers. His wife, Dolly, smiling so broadly that he could see her deep laughter lines, held up a coffee mug and came forward to look over his shoulder. It made him happy to see her looking so excited about the move and helped to dispel his sadness at the letter he had been reading. A new home in another country was a fitting beginning to a new millennium.

"It's cold in here now, and this is the last of the boxes. I'll take it indoors, and you can have a look," he said.

The box contained his father's paperwork. Not much of it, he had discovered, and in the main old bank statements and official documents from the so-called paperless age. But there was one thin plastic folder with a few poignant letters from Kieran to his granddad. He gave Dolly the letter which had so stirred up his remembrances of his father, and also of his own son, Kieran, at a reckless age.

Three generations; he thought. I wonder what my dad would have made of us going off to Australia to live. Bit of a patriotic die-hard, as he was.

After a brief surprised exclamation, when she saw the date on it – 28th February 1977 – Dolly read through the letter twice.

"This was all long before my time, John," she said, looking up at him with wide eyes. "I knew there was a crisis about Kieran when he was at Uni, but how did he get into such debt? Five thousand pounds, it says here! And when he tells his grandfather that he 'needs somewhere to hide'; that sounds scary. What on earth had happened and why didn't he come to you? You were not at loggerheads, were you? I had never got that impression."

"It was a lot of money, a hell of a lot in the seventies. My dad arranged a bridging loan and downsized to find enough to cover the debt for Kieran." He saw the flicker of horror in her eyes and her brow furrowing in disapproval. He could read her so well, although she always said the reverse was, in fact, the case. "Dad never told me about any of it until much later," he said. Which was true enough, and a watered down account at that.

"Go on, if you don't mind telling me," she said. "I realise it isn't any of my business and it is decades ago, but you *have* shown me the letter. Besides which, we owe Kieran so much. The house he has found for us in Sydney is splendid. Far more luxurious than we could have ever envisaged, even if you had designed it yourself, and I can't wait to get in it. I keep looking at the photos."

John sighed and put his empty coffee mug on the table. He sat back on the sofa and put his arms around her shoulder, gathering her in close against him. The rain was falling again; sheeting down the window, and the sky cast a strange, ominous orange-grey light. He blocked it all out with an image from sunny Australia at the Olympics last year. What a fantastic start to the new millennium that had been! The architectural impact of the freshness of the arenas, and all the energy, the grasping of ideas, technology, and hope for the future. It had impressed him tremendously during their visit. He remembered with a smile that the Australians had even successfully cloned a sheep! A namesake for my wife, Dolly, they had called it, and there had been lots of good-natured jokes about that.

"Kieran was always a bundle of energy and full of ideas, even as a young child," John said. "I can see him now at five or six, standing bolt upright in the middle of the kitchen, having abandoned his toys. He stood still, full of tension, with clenched fists, and stared into space. When I asked him what he was doing, he said, 'I have to make a plan!' Five years old, or perhaps six." John chuckled.

He gave Dolly a squeeze, and she responded by taking his hand and snuggled up closer. "Story-time," she said.

It was a reference to Dolly's frequent insomnia. She often had to cope with limited sleep. Especially when she was anxious, or had something on her mind. Sometimes, after tossing and turning for a while, she would ask him to tell her a story. They would be incidents from his past, a description of earlier periods in his life – he had travelled when younger – and she had told him to make the narrative as long-winded and boring as he could. Before he had exhausted the tale, she might fall asleep. What to tell her? John wondered. It was a complicated family history. He hoped he could give it justice and not make her sleepy as time approached for a cup of tea.

"Kieran had got in with some group or other in a speculative venture. It was a daft idea because he was a student and he did not have any money. God knows how he convinced them he wanted to be a part of it because I gathered they realised that. Anyway, it went wrong and everyone lost out. Hence, the debt and the threat he talks about in this letter he wrote." He took the sheet of *embossed* paper from Dolly and put it to one side. Another instance of Kieran's automatic instinct to find something which looked impressive to draw attention to his plight. The second part of John's explanation was more difficult.

"I don't know what I would have done if Kieran had turned to me, to be honest. It was the time when his mother had just got her final prognosis. She had not got long. I was not a powerful figure in his life because of what his mother was going through, which he refused to acknowledge, and he always got on well with his granddad." It sounded like an apology, perhaps that of a weak and derided man. Aspects of which were raw in his recollection of that time.

"I knew nothing about any of it until a long time afterwards. I have often thought that it may have shortened my dad's life. All that worry and how upsetting it was for him to have to move home, too. We are so lucky that our move is exciting and welcomed now that we can both retire, or not, as we choose."

"They kept you in the dark, the two of them, and that was their choice. There was nothing you could do about that. But your son, Kieran, *made good*, as they say," Dolly's response was cheerful. "Not only did he make a life for himself, but he is also the reason we are going to have a superb home and a lovely retirement in Australia. He's a very successful man, and only – what? In his early forties? There are exceptional years ahead for all of us, and no financial worries."

"Of course, you're right. I *know* it, but I don't always feel it," John said. He pointed to the box of papers on the floor. "I think I will just burn this lot. It's all irrelevant now. But do you think Kieran would like to have the letters to his granddad?"

"We could take them with us and offer them to him. Later on, though. Not on arrival. When we have settled in."

She looked puzzled and urged John to dig down his side of the sofa for the remote control. "Time for the news," Dolly said. "There was something on this morning about America … they are going into recession. That was about debt. Nothing for *us* to worry about."

Or was it? Didn't that mean a global effect on currency?

Could Kieran get them out of that problem if she raised it?

It was unlikely that Kieran could not cope with any eventuality. It would give John even more reason to forgive and forget. His son's burden in that he was responsible for the death of his grandfather, if he had occasioned it, was not John's fault.

By the time they arrived in Australia, the global financial crisis was all over the news, but Kieran assured them he had everything under control. It was only that he had pulled out of the house he had found them, for something smaller, or they could rent … and perhaps they could go on working, part time, for a few more years?

Dolly's lips tightened, and she restrained herself with a simple statement. "I think, John, you ought to show Kieran that letter now," she said.

THE GOAT'S SHOEHORN

It all began with the goat and inevitably she named him Billy. He was brown and white in random patches on his body and legs, but his head was distinctively brown on one side and white on the other. Sometimes she could guess his mood by which side of his face he presented to her. His ears were tufty and pale pink inside. His tail was a fluffy, white, curved brush.

The new house, new home, new country saga had taken over Alicia's life. The move to France was long awaited and exciting when it became a reality. Of course, she wanted it all to be perfect in double quick time. Money, of course, was the problem.

She had even caught Roger's enthusiasm for a Capability Brown approach to their field, which sloped to the river bank and three trees bordered the rough grass. Robert's plans were not as pretentious as they sounded when you studied the lay of the land. But the realisation of those ideas, scaled down, lay far ahead into the future.

"River frontage is the reason this property has so much potential," Roger had said. His eyes shone.

Did that asset cover up for the distressed and distressing state of the actual house? It would take their entire capital and a hefty loan to make it habitable and a home. At the time of Roger's eagerness to purchase the property, Alicia had gazed at it with plunging spirits as she studded the roof. "Sorry, Roger, but where exactly *is* the roof?" she asked. Adding, "Remind me again of how much we are paying for all this?" Though the field also distracted her with its possibilities.

While they waited for all the paperwork to go through, she admitted to an English neighbour that the potential of the land buoyed her. Her husband stressed a boating allusion and his plans for building a jetty. The land bordered the river for a short length.

Alicia had made few immediate decisions about the project, except that they could waste no money or labour on cutting back all the grass in the field. They would get a goat. That was the solution. Smiling at the thought, she pictured a young goat, and it seemed like another kind of lovable pet,

Alicia fell in love with the pygmy goat. He harvested grass, nettle, brambles and weeds at a steady rate, and he was good company. She often abandoned measuring up spaces, hod-carrying and cement-mixer filling tasks and instead, wandered down to the field to talk to Billy. He snuffled her hands for a delicacy and almost always received a tasty tit-bit. When Roger was getting on her nerves, she unburdened her exasperation by telling Billy all about it.

With weekends and evenings fully booked working on the house, and a job in the week, life shrank to eat, work, and sleep. *Métro, boulot, do do;* it sounded so much more poetic in French. Sometimes Alicia thought that only the goat could understand the tedium of it, but of course, Billy's life wasn't meant to be anything more than eat, sleep, work, if you considered that eating was also his work.

They dreamt of creating a kitchen garden over one season. It would be cheaper to grow their own vegetables. The loaned Rotavator churned up the soil and uncovered a rubbish dump by the side of the house.

It contained a great number of seafood shells, which revealed something of the eating habits of the previous owner. A French neighbour was quick to explain that they had only connected the hamlet to mains electricity in the fifties and rubbish collection by the commune waited for decades after that.

One morning, the same French neighbour alerted them in a feverish phone call. Billy was on the loose and picking off the heads of all their flowering plants. The flowers which Alicia had sown from seed or bulbs, hoping for a wonderful display in the coming months were all under threat.

The attempt to corner him and catch him with a lasso in which neither she nor Roger had developed sufficient skill continued for an hour, during which a crowd gathered to watch and give advice. Billy had to be tethered after that, and his freedom was more curtailed. The goat ate almost anything, but Alicia found him resting one sultry afternoon with a rejected object at his feet. Curious, she picked it up. It appeared to be made of bone, a scooped out shape, and had some carving or design scratched upon it. She cleaned it with water from the garden hose, and the more she handled it thereafter, the more she became convinced that it could be worth something.

"Scrimshaw. I think that's what it is. Like a scratchy sort of engraving. If it's old, it will be valuable, surely?"

Roger heard her musing, and lifted his gaze from his workbench to take a cursory look, but showed little interest after that.

Alicia's excitement was not quashed. The retrieved item had a certain shape, giving her the idea that they used it as a tool. In England, she had seen programmes on TV where such articles evoked surprise by their antiquity, and the experts gave estimates of extraordinary sums at auction.

"We're not making a trip back to the UK just for that," Roger said. He justified his negativity and enhanced it by the dismissive reaction to photographs of the object, which she emailed to friends, and also by the websites they explored.

As shorter winter days approached, they were busier than ever in making the house weatherproof and warm. Roger spent hours chopping wood. They envisaged a Christmas that would be bleak with finances so low. Although, Alicia had applied for another job and was on the short-list for an interview in the New Year, and friends offered generous hospitality for the season. New friends who remembered their own experiences when they were in the same position living in a foreign country, and they knew how hard it could be.

On a sudden inspiration, Alicia took the bone object to a local museum to see if they could identify it. Perhaps it was not a tool. Perhaps it was nothing other than a piece of well-hardened bone, which some animal had chewed, until the last tiny morsel of the flesh which once surrounded it was gone. Surely, it would be better to know if the find was special or not.

The official at the museum was instructive, if disappointing. The piece of bone was made of horn, and appropriately, she had joined in his laughter, thinking it obvious to him. Baffled, Alicia watched as the curator showed its use. It was not an ancient bone, and they had shaped it to form a shoe horn. It had some age, but not enough to be valuable.

"Well, at least we know now," Alicia said on her return home.

Roger gave her arm a squeeze. "Never mind, we'll get through. A real find would have been nice, but we *are* getting there." Alicia nodded an agreement and gave him a kiss in return.

It was still of use, of course, and Alicia placed the object by the shoe rack for employment in its correct purpose. When she dressed for the New Year interview, wearing a smart two-piece suit and new shoes, which were a bit too tight, she used it and dropped the shoe horn into her bag. She would drive in comfortable footwear and put the shoes on at the last possible moment. When the dreaded interview was over, she could at least be comfortable again on the journey home.

To her surprise, Alicia got the job. It was more money, fewer hours and greater prospects. Elated, she announced the good news to Robert. Before he opened a bottle of wine to finish with supper, she hurried down the lane and into the field, looking for the goat. She had a tit-bit with her. Alicia told the goat of her good fortune, patted his head, avoiding his yellowing teeth, and thanked him for finding the shoe horn for her. Now she regarded it as her personal talisman. To what else might it bring a welcome stroke of luck?

A PLAY ON WORDS

Jack Hornby puffed on his cigar. Of course, it *appeared* to defy all the strictures on smoking, but it was only herbal and rather disgusting, no matter how hard the manufacturers had tried to fool the olfactory sensors. As he billowed out smoke, he contemplated the despatch of his latest masterpiece and pressed the buzzer just once, – only a squeak – to summon his secretary, Sweet Pea. He bullied her, but she retaliated with equal ferocity and was taller, and more robustly built than he was. She had past form in the sport of shot put.
"Time to awaken that lot across the pond," he said. She had arrived and come to a halt, standing towering in front of his desk, with arms folded across her chest. An athlete's absence of bosoms, he always noted, but would never comment on or even allude to her appearance. "Check my flight time again … please*,* Sweet Pea." His smile was an appeasing one.

****

In England, Carol opened the bound manuscript again. The first time had been with a caress for the gilded edges to the pages, and a serene moment or two had followed, admiring the copperplate writing within. This 'original' manuscript, of which there were several, an expensive printer had prepared as an archive copy of the author's work. The playwright was in the classical mode, well-established and carrying much kudos. These manuscripts, and she did not know how many they had produced, were all made to impress, and they did so. Carol's task was to type it out and make the usual ordinary copies for the company. She had already done most of it.

Everyone now knew who the author was and that he had once been a local, helped to explain why he had chosen their amateur dramatic society. That and the possession of the fine theatre which their small market town could boast. Their recollections and stories about the writer in his youth had poured forth at the last meeting of the group. They had discussed his fame and reputation. Carol had added her own memories to other, often disparaging accounts. However, the generous figure with several zeros that Jack Hornby had allocated for the entire production was more than ample compensation for disagreement.

Early that morning, between weekend chores, Carol had made notes about the play on the A4 pad headed by the logo of the charity fund she supported. Since then, she had read through it, mulled it all over, and almost finished the work. Picking up an eraser, which she twiddled for a moment, she gazed out at the orange glow of the evening sunset. She had inserted some slight adjustments and ideas about costumes which appealed to her.

*****

"Can we double up on some of these parts? Think about it. They only have a few lines, some of them." Derek looked around the table and stabbed at the sheaf of stapled pages, already falling apart and needing punch holes and treasury tags, or string. He would have a word with Carol. Always practical, he had concentrated on reading the cast list and ignored the increasing bubble of chatter as the drama group continued leafing through their copies. He wanted them to focus. Make a start. Connie only got walk-on parts and could recognise those. Bored, she studied each face around the trestle table as they got ready for the first reading. *Coffee and biscuits at eleven. Must put the hot water on,* she thought. "Has everyone read it right through? I didn't get it at all," she said, and repeated the question, timorously raising her voice.

Connie's neighbour, Timothy, turned towards her, lowering his voice. "People don't, do they? Get it, I mean. It's highbrow – you know, sophisticated stuff. Meant to be." He was looking down the table at their director. However, Derek was deep in conversation with the props man.

It doesn't do to be negative, or you'd never get a leading-man's role, Timothy thought. *Or was that only what they called it in films?* It was Timothy's first play with the group.

Derek had a large auctioneer's hammer, and he rapped it on the table to quieten them down and it soon pierced the zenith of their conversations. "I'm going to allocate parts," he said, waving a raised hand at the immediate antagonistic reaction. "Only for this first reading. We can change it all later." He ploughed on through his list, ticking off each character, to which he had added the initials of a group member. Narrator, knight, cavalier, jurist … It was a period piece, well not exactly, as far as he could tell. Not a well-known play, but intended as a young playwright's nod to Shakespeare? Hamlet? One of the History plays? Julius Caesar?

"We need livery costumes for the lord's servants. I've got nothing suitable at all," the props man intervened. His voice was not much more than a quaver. "Oh, and a shovel. But someone will have one for gardening, I expect. I haven't got a garden." He put a smoothing hand to his temple to comfort an intransigent headache. He wore a thick jersey and had a heavy cold.

"How about a break for tea? You put the water on, Connie?" Hermione stood up, and everyone soon followed suit. They always did. "While we're on the subject, Derek," Hermione said, blocking his pathway to the tea, "we need at least something temporary for the kitchen area backstage. Waterproofing. That damn urn leaks like a sieve. Plasterboard, perhaps. Gypsum is waterproof ..."

Derek took his tea to a quiet corner, leaving Hermione to supervise the biscuits, and beckoned Carol. She edged her way towards him, not knowing what to expect.

"That costume list, Carol. Are you OK with that? Looks complicated."

"Not too difficult, Derek. I've got a source. Morris dancers in Lostwithiel use something like them, so I've heard."

"I wonder what made Jack think of them, though." Derek frowned.

"Well, as we've all discussed, he was a *local* boy, and still has contacts. Perhaps he's heard how good we are, too?" Carol smiled and sipped her mug of tea.

"And the scenery ... difficult to visualise," Derek said.

"We *can* do it, of course."

"I should think so. There isn't much of it." Carol sounded terse and pursed her lips.

What was on her mind was nothing to do with their competence, only the remembrance, brought to light, of all Jack's slights, pomposity, and worse. Well, there was an opportunity for revenge.

****

Jack jammed his finger down on the buzzer for Sweet Pea. He had had little sleep.

She took her time, having listened for the thud of another dart. That would be Hitchcock again, then. Jack had photos of famous producers, film and stage, on one wall opposite the desk in his office. They acted as a frame on an axis surrounding an enormous flattering portrayal of his *own* fine features – from a few decades ago. The darts always holed the Hitchcock photo the most. Sweet Pea had to replace it from time to time.

"To what do I owe this pleasure, Jack? I'm on my coffee break, you know."

The tone had a definite edge, and he took it as a warning. "Got little sleep, Sweet Pea," he ventured in a whine, but then abandoned it. "Have you had a look at the Webcam recording? And are there any reviews yet?" he demanded.

"Time difference, Jack." She pointed at the digital wall space showing the time in major cities all over the world. He didn't understand it, but it looked super professional and as though he was in great demand. "Yes, I have had a look at the recording of the first night," Sweet Pea added.

"Well? Is it good? They're only amateurs, you know."
"I think you need to take a look for yourself. I've set it up for you in the cinema. I'll bring in the reviews as soon as …" Sweet Pea turned her broad back on him and walked out, head erect. It was a physical rebuff, a metaphorical turning up of the nose.

Jack had a bad feeling. He located it in his gut. He flipped the lights on in the cinema room, started up the recording from the control panel, and watched, bedazzled, in dumb confusion for a while. This was his play, and he hoped they had not made a complete mess of it. It was an honour for the amateur drama group to be doing it. Accolades for them.

It was the screaming, and the sound of his kicking feet on the short row of sumptuous, ergonomic seats in the cinema that brought Sweet Pea forth from where she had hidden nearby.

"What the …. Fff … flipping hell are they wearing?" he shouted when he saw her.

"I did a bit of research, Jack. It ain't American, I can tell you that. It's a fashion, I think; the goggles, monocles, and long leather coats, telescopes, pistols, and lots of black. And that's just the men. They call it Steampunk."

Jack's face was burgundy red, verging on purple, and his open mouth displayed its collected spittle. He was speechless and grabbed at the tilted back of a damaged seat for support.

"I followed the script and they haven't changed that much," Sweet Pea said. He must have looked sick, because her tone was almost sympathetic.

Jack collapsed into the seat. "Bring me a whisky, Sweet Pea. A large one."

"Take some deep breaths." Those were Sweet Pea's parting words, and she didn't even comment on the lack of a 'please' to make the whisky a request.

Jack looked up at the screen. He held a hand over his eyes, to curb the impact of what he saw, and waited until Sweet Pea returned.

While gulping whisky, he paused to remind his secretary, or perhaps himself, that his play portrayed 'a sophisticated parody, a metaphysical allusion or comparison with the 17th century English civil war, regarding the aspect of the conflict of the class system – titles, versus a growing democratic of merchant trade and money ....' Sweet Pea zoned out, not impressed. It sounded intellectual, but she knew he had learned it by heart from a review.

Jack held a hand to his chest, to still the erratic, over-swift beating of his heart.

"Look!" he mouthed, and gestured at the scene still rolling in front of their eyes. "The backdrop scenery … is that a STEAM train?"

Suddenly, he halted and listened again. There was laughter and a burst of applause. The webcam had swivelled onto the audience, and they looked absorbed, joyful, clutching at each other in their hilarity, but completely involved in the play. This was not, he realised, such a bad response to the performance. Jack calmed down further.

"I didn't know you did comedy, Jack," Sweet Pea said. She was smiling, too, looking at all those smiling faces in the audience.

A DROP TOO MUCH

So much to do. Another fun-filled day in his life. Of course, he loved it, except for those last instructions from the King, the Master of the Universe! Well, he wasn't, of course, but he **was** named after the outermost, major moon of the planet Uranus.

I should never have told Oberon that about the planet with his own name; Robin thought. It went to his head. Well, it would; he's vainglorious, swelled with pride. A bighead, in fact, although small in body.

Fortunately, I gave him some distraction, too, with the fact of his magnificence, since Titania is always carping about something or other at the moment and they keep quarrelling. Pretty, but mean, that one, with her adoring coterie of fairies. I quite fancy Pease-blossom now Moth is ignoring me, and I am determined to give up on that one. Whereas, my master needed something to hold over his queen, even if it's only his name. When I told him about the connection, it raised his spirits, and he overlooked a few things I had done not so well. He still called me a knave, but added I was shrewd. Which is complimentary, isn't it?

What's in a name, anyway? Mine is *Good fellow* and I certainly do not live up to that!

Those two are fun to watch; he thought. Oberon has a plan now to humiliate Titania. She refused to give up a changeling he wanted for a knight or henchman; he told me, because the child's mother was one of Titania's devotees. He is preparing a trick to play on her to do with an ass. It made me laugh when he called his queen a flibbertigibbet and said that she was fickle. So, he intends to make her look the epitome of foolishness. I can't wait to see what he does. She makes it obvious that she does not like me and told me to keep away from her fairies.

Robin sighed. It was almost dusk in the forest, and he had been waiting all day for the moment to complete this chore for Oberon. Earlier today, it had been bright, with the white bridal bouquets of May flowers, which seemed fitting now for what he was about to do. Those two, the man and the woman, had settled down below to sleep on the soft mossy grass, he noticed, which would make his task easier. They were quiet and unaware.

There had already been enough confusion between these two and another pair of humans. Oberon had intervened and insisted they had to sort it out. So all four must fall asleep, forgetting what had happened, and then the correctly administered love potion could restore the four young people's proper relationships to each other.

'No mistakes!' Oberon had warned.

Robin was weary and needed to get the job over with so that he could settle down himself for the night. He yawned and moved closer, getting into position right above the couple below.

He had meant to flutter and float like a butterfly, not be stung like a bee! But found that the gossamer green tunic he wore had strangled his thighs like an overwrought columbine. It forced him to hover at an unnatural angle as he dripped the potion liberally over the humans' sleeping eyes, and he saw one glassy droplet miss its mark. He held up a finger to test the breeze. It seemed to be in a reasonable trajectory for the task.

The woman shifted, curled up a little tighter. He listened and waited. Not a whisper in the dusky glade, so he judged it would be alright, and the planned aim would work. He retreated from the sleeping forms and flew straight up above them.

Settling himself inside the unfurled leaf of the nearest branch of a chestnut tree, whose fruit and leaves splayed conveniently upwards, Robin watched and waited for a while. The couple's breathing slowed, and their mouths slackened.

He was grateful for that because a hooting owl had already warned of Robin's presence. Although, would humans even recognise that? He watched the golden, shimmering spread of sunset in the canopy above as the events of the day passed before his sleepy eyes. He had spent much of it looking for that flower, *love in idleness*, which changes colour from white to purple when struck by Cupid's arrow. It contained a magical juice, which Oberon intended to use on Tatiana's sleeping eyelids. It was all part of his trick to humiliate her.

Robin had used the flower, which held the same substance, on the couple sleeping below. Its beaded pearls induced love.

He laughed at the memory of the other projects he had achieved that day. "Ho ho ho," he chuckled, but the sound was tiny, a tinkle, and undetectable by human ears. He was thinking of the surprise on the gossip's face, as her bum slipped from the stool he had pulled out from under her and then replaced. The vigour of his amusement made him rock his fiery head and increased the unpleasant aching sensation in his temples which he could not dispel. A reminder that there was another pleasure he had indulged in during the late afternoon – drinking an outstanding quantity of nectar, even for him.

He crossed his legs and forced himself to lie still, permitting only a slight movement of his body, and thus subduing the throbbing in his head. He raised his feet to admire the up-turned points of his dazzling, colourful slippers. A distraction which brought to mind Peaseblossom because she had woven them for him. The pain soon dulled, and he closed his eyes in a deep, immersing sleep.

*****

Robin awoke to the sound of rude words. Embittered voices criss-crossed the early morning trills of the birds.

"You goat! I hate the very sight of your misshapen face! Get away from me!"

"Call me a goat? You wretched hag! I wouldn't touch you if they paid me."

Robin jumped upright, dispersing a drop of dew from his flattened leaf, and gazed below. The woman had her arm raised to strike, and not for the first time, judging by the red streak on her lover's cheek. Her face distorted in ugly fury; her mouth agape as she let out a loud and strident shriek. The man backed away, but only to restrain his own fist from landing a blow. Meanwhile, she bent to pick up a fallen branch and what was she going to do next?

It was all getting too much to bear. Robin blocked his ears. What must he do? No more mess. They should be enamoured, not fighting. He had done nothing wrong!

I have made no mistake! A love potion cannot cause this ... chaos. Oberon will have my guts for garters!

Robin could not believe it was happening. In desperation, he made to pinch his own arm. It was a tremendous relief that he felt nothing, not even when he tried a second time.

He sat back on his knees, his pointed slippers scraping a hole in the leaf, and a frightening dark chasm opened ... and then closed.

Of course – too much nectar drunk yesterday afternoon. This would never happen in real life. It's all just a dream; A Midsummer Night's Dream.

He closed his eyes and returned to his dream in which Pease-Blossom was the prominent feature.

<u>With thanks to Wikipedia</u>

Oberon, also designated Uranus IV, is the outermost major moon of the planet Uranus. It is the second-largest and second most massive of the Uranian moons, and the ninth most massive moon in the Solar System.

(So, the King of the fairies had good reason for his big head!)

Robin Goodfellow is also known as Puck.

AN AFFLICTION OF THE EYE

"Sarah! I didn't expect to see you today. See? Joke! Rather a poor one, you will no doubt think," said Anne as Sarah entered the hospital room. Sarah saw Anne turning with effort onto her side in the bed in order to face the open door.

Moving towards the bed, a cellophane bouquet of mixed roses obscuring her face, Sarah glanced around the private room in the clinic. Light and airy, an enormous window with the blinds closed against the glare. But a soft light from a ceiling-fitting revealed a bedside table cluttered with cards, others pinned on a pegboard by the bed, and an expensive television screen on the opposite wall. To one side of the bed, she saw a wheelchair, and to the other an armchair.

Thank goodness. This is a secure and comfortable space for her; Sarah thought. All she knew was that her former friend was suffering both physically and mentally.

Anne accepted a kiss on her right cheek. Her face was bandaged and padded down one side. Sarah tried not to wince at what she imagined lay beneath. Her coal-black hair, which curved into her neck at chin length, had been washed and styled, and the hands which lifted the roses to her face were manicured. These were encouraging signs. Sarah remembered how Anne had always cherished her fingernails.

"Have they any perfume? These hothouse roses usually don't," said Anne. She did not find out and offered them back to Sarah. "Someone will put them in water." Her voice was hoarse, as though unused.

Sarah moved the flowers to one side of the bed. "How are you feeling?"

"It isn't painful." Anne touched the padding with one finger. "Except when they remove the dressings." She hunched her shoulders in a dismissive shrug. "What have *you* been up to?"

Sarah did not linger on that first occasion; she

had been told ten minutes, and she surreptitiously checked her watch, although she did not need to worry, as the nurse returned while she was taking her leave of Anne; no doubt to remove her. To her surprise, outside in the corridor, the nurse beckoned her on to the nurses' station. "You're old friends, I believe?"

"Well, yes. We hadn't been in touch for a long time. We date back to school days, really. It was Anne's daughter, Fiona, who contacted me about where she was."

The nurse nodded. "I'm Margaret, just call me Margaret." They shook hands.

"You are coming back, then?" the nurse asked.

"Of course. Anything I can do to help, I'll be pleased to do." Sarah had questions to ask, but did not feel able to pose them, not at that moment. "I thought I might visit a couple of afternoons each week. I have the free time."

"Good. Try to get her to talk about it. What happened, I mean. You *know,* don't you?"

57

Margaret had turned away to some paperwork on her desk, then looked back at Sarah's blank face. "Never mind, for now. Dr Gregson is helping her. You could talk to him, perhaps, on another visit." She smiled and opened the door. "You know your way out?"

Sarah's regular visits stretched out over several weeks, and the periods spent with Anne increased in length. Sarah was pleased to feel the trust and intimacy had returned between them, step-by-step. At first, she had been shocked and distressed at the changes she saw in her old school friend.

On one grey, wintry afternoon's visit, Anne was ready to tell her what had happened. As Sarah came in, Anne sat up straight in the armchair, with an air of purpose. She picked up a cane painted with a white strip resting against the side of the chair. Anne fingered the top of the cane, clasped the rounded top, then splayed her fingers wide open and rested her palm against it.

"Problems with balance. I have to learn to walk again!" Anne explained with the semblance of a laugh. She continued to repeat the series of splaying actions with her right hand. She motioned for Sarah to perch on the side of the bed and drew in a deep breath.

"You know I work from home a lot? On my hard drive computer," Anne began. Sarah nodded. She knew Anne had worked in interior design for several years after her divorce and had a prosperous business. "Well, that's where it all started." Anne nodded her head as if to emphasise the point.

"I was sitting in my study early one morning, writing an e-mail to a potential client. I had only typed two lines and turned my head to check a design printout which was rustling off the printer."

Anne drew in a noisy rasp of breath, and it made Sarah jump a little.

"As my gaze moved back to the screen, a gradual pixelating image formed beneath the typed words. It resolved." Anne paused and licked her dry lips. "It showed a single, open eye."

Anne's head dipped, and then she raised

herself up again and looked towards the window opposite her. A distraction, or to gather strength? Sarah wondered.

"At that time, the large, black pupil of that eye appeared to be focussing on an object over to my left," said Anne.

"I have to describe it to you."

"The iris, deep-blue on the outer ring, was mottled with feathery white lines … that part was rather beautiful." She paused and blinked her undamaged eye. "But from the pinkness of the lower eyelid, projected thick clumps of the embedded, brown roots of eyelashes. Those obscene lashes offended and nauseated me by their magnification in which the eye itself did not." Anne moistened her dry lips with her tongue. "I saw that some shadow had fallen on the top eyelid, which obscured the detail of those lashes, and covered them with a matt brownness, which looked fleshy, moist and was – repellent."

"I checked my toolbar. I could see no sign of the image being an import from another document, so I highlighted it and deleted it."

60

"The following morning, the eye was there again. I tried a screen shot. Nothing appeared on that. It was blank."

The tone and speed of Anne's speech, which had begun in almost flippant asides, changed to a lowered huskiness; faltering, punctuated by deep, breathy intakes of air, and sudden breaks in the narrative, when her grip tightened on the cane until the fingers turned a bloodless white, and she moved her head and neck as if to jerk her back into the tale.

"The image continued to appear, enlarging like a growing cell. It drew me to it. Was it male or female, young or old? Even when I re-booted my computer, I could not remove the eye. It stayed on the screen.

"It convinced my daughter, Fiona, that it was some kind of cookie. She never saw it herself. I told Gerald about it. He is a computer geek and came to my house to look at my system, but found nothing. He left me so aware that he had been looking for something for the existence of which I had no real, tangible evidence!"

Anne stabbed the cane down against the floor. Was it in anger or frustration?

"I was having difficulty sleeping. My doctor prescribed some sleeping pills and insisted I had my eyes tested. Then when they did not work and my optician said my eyes were fine, I bought a new screen. It made no difference. On another critical day, I searched and found a computer engineer who could download my precious files onto a new hard drive. I was considering wiping out everything on there, including all my precious designs.

"My birthday passed without celebration and the continuous horrible image fogged my mind with strange phrases and expressions. I still have those words in my head." Anne chanted the words so low that it was almost inaudible.

Seeing is not always believing.

The eyes are the mirror of the soul

"When the computer engineer left on that day,

I was so on edge that I flinched at his parting words – 'I have left it switched on for you. It's ready.' It unnerved me."

"I ran a hot bath. After that, I sat on the bathroom chair and I creamed and pushed down my cuticles, which was a deliberate distraction of sorts. I picked up the nail scissors and trimmed some minute slivers from these finger nails." Anne raised one hand and splayed the fingers towards Sarah.

"Wrapped in my towelling robe, I walked into my study, unable to delay any further."

Sarah watched in alarm as Anne's whole body shook.

"The eye had changed!" Her words came out in a high-pitched wail. "It was hideous, and it glared at me. The white was black. From the tear duct trickled rage-red daggers. Then it tilted, the focus moved." She raised a hand to her face.

"I felt the scissors in my hand, and I mouthed the words … "Anne's voice cracked. "If thine eye offends thee, pluck it out!" Tears streamed down one cheek, and she gave an agonising, open-mouthed moan.

"How could I do it, Sarah? The pain … help me! Help me!" Anne's head fell forward, and she collapsed, crumpled in the chair.

Sarah jumped up. Her own nails were digging into her closed fists, and she had drawn blood on her palms. She ran out into the corridor to the nurse. "Margaret, Margaret, come quickly!"

64

CHAIN OF EVENTS

'Hold on tight! Just hold on!' The cry came from in front of me.

Did I brace myself? I have no idea. The next thing I knew the tandem had veered at a horrible angle towards the narrow grass verge, skidded to a stop, and my leg hurt. Extracting myself from the saddle and unwrapping my limbs from the metal frame of the bike took all my concentration.

The white van with a red stripe, which had forced us off the road, had already sped on before I was even aware of what had happened. Tony, my husband, helped me to stand up. He looked unhurt, just mud splashed and, although he would never admit it, shaken. He shouted a few choice words down the Romney Marsh lane leading away into the distance and assured me he was fine.

A trickle of blood crept down my leg and I unhooked my bag from the carrier zipped onto the bike and rummaged around for tissues. We had a small first aid kit, but I could see it would not need that.

The worst of it was that we had no idea where we were. We had strayed from familiar byways, trying to take a short-cut because of the impending storm, and only knew we were heading in the right direction to return to Peasmarsh and our parked car.

I stood upright and peered around. Tony had righted the tandem, propped it against a bramble thicket and left me to advance on foot to see if he could get our bearings. The sky loomed in the interesting shape of a battleship grey cloud, with ominous rolling edges and a bulbous black section in the middle. I watched, mesmerised, as it drifted further towards us. I am going to ache tomorrow; I thought, and there will be the usual extraordinary colourful bruises to follow.

It was not the first time we had been caught in rain, of course, even torrential rain, and I dragged out the long wet-weather jackets with their hoods, which were rolled up tight inside the small carrier. My hands were cold and clumsy in the task. Although it was not the first time the weather had caught us out, I had never experienced being thrown off the bike before.

It had been an inspiring day out up until then. We had explored new terrain that morning and covered about 20 miles already. This was exceptional for our first ride of the year in the early spring. After a brief pub visit for a light snack and a draught beer, we had only stopped again when I spotted an old derelict house. Part of the corrugated roof was off, but the name 'Elmhurst' appealed, as we soft pedalled by, and I told Tony that it made me think of a horror film. I wanted to investigate.

It was a pre-fabricated building used long after the end of the war and not a crumbling mansion with potential for hauntings.

'I want to stop to look inside. I wonder when it was abandoned and what sort of people lived here last?'

Tony was used to my curiosity and knew I could never resist a ruin of any description. 'There's a lot of nettles and scrub,' he warned.

'I'll see if we can get in around the back.'

There was a badly bloated dead sheep around the back, and he did not want me to follow. I am not that squeamish though, and we soon found a door jammed back and slightly open.

Inside the single storey house there was nothing left but the flimsy partitioned walls. You could work out the functions of the rooms: the marks from a dresser in the kitchen and the blackened fireplace. One room had scraps of faded wallpaper and I knew instantly from the teddy bear design that it was a child's room. Amongst the leaf mould on the floor of another area were strewn sheets from sixties and seventies magazines. All of them seemed to be articles on children's education. I bent down and retrieved a few torn pages.

'She was a teacher, then,' I said. 'I wonder why she left these behind. I hope she moved to something better – a modern, well- built house, instead of this isolated lean to.' I dropped abandoned pages to the floor, feeling sad, and hurried out of the door, down the dry weed-filled curve of a stone path, and onto the tarmac road. We left the ruin and continued to cycle on in silence.

I was drawn back into the present suddenly, as Tony appeared from his investigations in the rain after our tumble from the bike. It broke off my thoughts about the changing fortunes of the day. I saw him running from round a curve in the lane.

'I think we might find some shelter,' he said. He lifted up the bike to check the chain. 'There's a bloke further round that bend and he was beckoning us on. He waved at me. I think there is another pub near here.'

A few drops of rain hit my face and quickly turned into a stream, so I shook out a jacket to unravel it, and thrust it at Tony, before I struggled into my own. We mounted the tandem and pedalled away.

In the far distance, peering through heavy rain in gloomy light, I could just see the man Tony had mentioned gesturing to the right. He disappeared from view as we drew closer, no doubt taking shelter himself.

To our great relief, shortly afterwards we spotted a pub sign swinging by the gate of a pretty garden furnished with rain sodden wooden tables and benches. Far more important was the small building, which lay behind and back from the lane, and showed a light through the open door of a porch. We approached, hearing voices from the bar, and soon sniffed the welcoming, hoppy smell of beer mingling with that of wet coats and wax jackets. We removed our own outer clothing, shook off the rain, and added ours to the stack hanging on a line of pegs.

The pub turned out to be one of those period places. Memorabilia of the Second World War covered the walls. They only served alcohol, no food, and the beer was limited to only a couple of brews. As we drained our first glass of malty beer, we learned from the photographs on the walls that old Doris, the landlady, was a former land army girl.

Though we had been eyed and noted on arrival, as strangers often are in a pub which mainly serves a local community, we were so relieved to find a refuge from the weather that this did not affect us. Not at first.

'This is medicinal as much as anything else.' Tony joked as he asked for a second round. 'We were catapulted into the verge back there by some idiot in a white van!'

I joined in. 'White van with a red stripe. It looked like some kind of emergency vehicle – which we might have done with! It shook *me* up, anyway.'

Doris looked away, but not before I saw a frown deepen the creases on her face and lips pursed into a taut slit. A hush had descended. A young woman with long black hair came up to us from the other end of the bar and dealt with our order.

I swung Tony round by his free arm and encouraged him towards a seat in a corner. 'What on earth did we say wrong? I lowered my voice into almost a whisper. 'Did you notice the reaction?'

'God knows,' he said. Tony rubbed the smeared glass on the steamed-up window. 'The rain is easing off. We will go soon.'

While we gulped our beers the normal low

pub chatter started up again.

Before we had finished and carried our glasses back to the bar, the young woman with black hair, who had served us, made her way over to our table and sat down beside us. 'Sorry about that,' she said. 'We none of us mean to be rude. Not what you do with customers anyway, is it? You touched on a sore point that is all.'

I studied her long nose and strong jaw and warmed to her easy smiling expression. She looked friendly now.

'Are you related to Doris, by any chance? Only I can see resemblances, I think. She is a remarkable lady, judging by the photos.'

'Well, you are not wrong there. I am her granddaughter.'

She leaned in towards me. 'Did you see anyone else on your way here? I wanted to ask.'

'My husband saw a man who … he sort of directed us here. But I don't know – it was

72

raining so hard and came over so dark.'

'That' will be him, then,' she said. She nodded her head. 'You're not the first.'

I noticed her folded hands clasped in her lap as she raised her gaze, paused, and sighed.

'It was all long ago. Doris's daughter was killed on that lane, you see. Knocked down by a tractor. On a day like this ….' The young woman pointed outside the window at the grey wintry afternoon. 'A stranger came to help her – someone on a walking holiday or summat. He got help and they saved the baby she was carrying … but not Rose herself. She was an unlucky one, my mum. I would not be here meself, if he hadn't saved me. I was that baby.' She breathed heavily and turned away.

'God, how awful. What a tragedy.'

'Yes, it was for me and my gran. The worst of it is that it's all long ago now, and I never knew my mum, but gran still remembers it like yesterday.'

Something suddenly troubled me, and I had to

ask. 'What did Rose, your mother, do? Did she have a job locally ... somewhere around here, I mean?'

'Teacher, she was. Lived up on the marshes. Doris was always very proud of her.'

DAMASK ROSES

Heritage Day. How Laura hated it. They had been members of the Historic Roses group for decades, and how quickly the calendar arrived to this point. She gazed out across the lawn from the sitting-room window, closed now for privacy despite the warm sunshine of the June afternoon, and watched people's heads bending down to inhale into the heart of the blooms. Heads bobbing up and down and backs arching with stiffness afterwards, as the visitors to their garden wove an erratic path.

Not that their garden was enormous, nor were the varieties grown there extensive. It would all be over in half an hour, and she could hear the clatter in the conservatory of Susan, her daughter, as she prepared cups and saucers for the tea and buns. The WI group, with their stubby biros and questions, would soon consume them.

Laura rehearsed the introduction she must give and spoke the first few sentences aloud to the room. 'The roses came to Europe in the

Middle Ages from the Middle East, via Damascus – hence their name. However, it was not until the 16th century that a form of damask rose was first noted, which flowered *more than once ...*' her voice trailed away.

The Autumn Damask, as they knew it in England, she thought, and hopefully they were nearing the winter for this collection.

Laura had never appreciated the musky perfume; too earthy for her tastes, and it made her think of the great unwashed. She preferred a light, clean citrus smell like the scent she always bought and wore, which left only an ephemeral trace.

The roses were her husband's passion, not hers. Over the years, she had helped in every aspect of their cultivation. Endless cold November and February afternoons of precision pruning had been the worst. Even though she protested, their circle of friends saw her as the model wife supporting her husband's hobby. The rose-related holidays abroad had offered some surprising and welcome escape; she had drifted off to the intriguing centre of some walled town occasionally, while her husband climbed on a tour coach, clasping an informative plan and timetable. Those hours spent apart allowed her to draw breath.

Late retirement from a demanding career, and a series of debilitating minor ailments, meant that he had to spend more time indoors with his books and his newspaper. Laura often found him asleep with a rose catalogue spread open on his knees. But at other times his silhouette appeared at the sitting-room window, with his binoculars trained on her and the roses as she tried to follow all his minute instructions for each season's maintenance work. She knew what to do, but it was never to his standard. He tried to restrain his concern.

Sometimes he would open a window against the damp air and call down the garden, through cupped hands. 'Sorry, love. Laura! Can you hear me? Open that one up more at the base – let the air circulate!' Then, as she stooped with the cutters, the squeaking sound of the window closed against draughts. Her mood spoiled by the niggling warning that the hinges on the window needed attention, too.

77

After the completion of the season's cycle, when that year had passed, she initiated something she had already decided. If Robert would not relinquish his obsession, then she must employ sabotage as the solution. She knew how to keep the roses free from black spot and the more serious fungal diseases; powdery mildew and canker, leaf larvae and root borers, but she also had the skill to induce an insidious, at first, gradual, decline in the shrubs.

While she noted her successes with hope for the future, and regret for the past, she countered Robert's initial dismay by astute questions, leading him on to what they both knew; roses had a limited life in even the best locations. The wholesale replacement of the rose collection was a gargantuan task and quite beyond them now.

In the early spring, she had other more personal concerns. At first, they seemed minuscule, and even ludicrous. Her toenails, which had hardened and discoloured with age, distorted and twisted in shape. Standing became painful. Her chiropodist cut them back with difficulty, remarking on their sharp points.

One morning, Laura awoke to find scratched runnels of dried blood on the calves of her legs. After that, she wore socks in bed and applied thick slippery creams to guard her irritated skin from wounds insensibly inflicted by her feet. The socks, pierced with holes, she discarded and renewed.

To her dismay, the scent of musk roses, no longer in bloom in the garden, seemed to emanate more and more strongly from her own body. She took frequent showers, soaked for long periods in baths of astringent salts, but the heavy odour always returned.

As the year drew on, she removed the blackened stems of the dead rose bushes – a notable, if sad success – dropping them into a pile she had covered with a thick plastic square, which was normally used as a cover to prevent the growth of weeds. One long border was now denuded and barren.

Climbing out of the bath in the evenings, she grabbed a towelling robe and by patting let the moisture absorb into it. She could not towel herself dry by rubbing with vigour, in the usual way. Her skin became tinged a deeper pink blush as its vulnerable softness broke inexplicably into painful splits.

One sunny but chilly afternoon, she stood on the dusty grey expanse of crumbled soil and stooped to pick up some remnants of green gardening string. Horrified, she felt something seize her legs and twine itself around them, like roots twisting through the earth in a time lapse film, or plant stalks winding around a cane. She pulled up one side of her fleece-lined trousers and looked in alarm at a long, unnatural, brown vein running from her knee to the ankle. She gazed, fascinated, at its raised appearance, which seemed to writhe. For a threatening moment, she could not move, unable to lift her feet in their mud-proof, green rubber overshoes.

Laura returned to the house, limping across the patchy grass in the moss covered lawn. From initial nervous laughter, she gasped and coughed at the thought that the roses were fighting back!

Panting with effort, she paused at the back door, looked down the entire length of the desolate, denuded garden, and wondered gravely how she could atone for what she had done to the roses, and to Robert who missed them so.

Nobody knows this little Rose by Emily Dickinson

Nobody knows this little Rose --
It might a pilgrim be
Did I not take it from the ways
And lift it up to thee.
Only a Bee will miss it --
Only a Butterfly,
Hastening from far journey --
On its breast to lie --
Only a Bird will wonder --
Only a Breeze will sigh --
Ah Little Rose -- how easy
For such as thee to die!

NIGHT DRINKERS

(Inspired by Nighthawks painting by Edward Hopper (1942)

"No more for you. You've had enough!"

A couple of heads swivelled at the sound of the raised voice, drinks poised and conversation halted. Trouble? Something to break the monotony, then. Something to talk about when you've exhausted work, the car and the wife; Tom thought. Not that the bar was raucous and echoing with conversation. In fact, only a few 'singles' lined this side of the long L-shaped bar. Balanced on their bar stools, they stared morosely at their drinks. Early in the evening yet.

82

Tom watched as the burly, red-faced barman put his heavy hand on the young man's shoulder and propelled him towards the door. He did not resist.

'What's he done then? Who is he?' asked Tom hoarsely of his nearest neighbour.

Thirty years old, thin and known for the chesty cough which kept erupting from his stooped frame, Tom was still in his city suit, but with a loosened tie, and he was on his way home. He watched the offender being hauled to the door, as he pulled his camel coat closer and wrestled with the buttons.

An expensive-looking coat, but well-worn now, Tom thought. He followed the young man's retreating back until the final push by the bartender which placed him outside the pub. Then Tom got a reply to his query.

"That's Mike. He's always here on Thursdays. Seen him before, haven't you? Surely to God! This often happens. He'll be standing outside on the corner opposite now."

Tom turned away from the man who spoke

and also wafted stale, beery breath into his own face. How long had *he* been drinking? But the incident raised Tom's interest. Today had begun as boring and ended up as stressful. He didn't want to think about what had happened today and so he welcomed a distraction.

"Mike? Mike who?" he asked. "Is he a regular, then?"

"Barman's son, of course," the beery man said. He jabbed with one forefinger of his left hand, which was wrapped, as though glued, to his own glass, at the returning barman. Some of the liquid in the glass slopped against the side, but the glass was almost empty.

The flushed barman knocked his thigh against a table and winced as he strode back in haste to the bar. He lifted the hinged flap of the counter and, when back in position, he took a quick glance around the empty tables, seeming to weigh them up. Bending towards Tom's informative neighbour, the barman spoke to him in an undertone. "Got to change a barrel. Keep an eye on things. OK?" He turned aside at once, in response to an affirmative nod, and disappeared out the back.

"Stands outside in the rain … for hours, some nights," Tom's neighbour muttered.

Tom gathered he was referring to the ousted young man and not the barman. Those blots of white on the barman's son's coat, Tom thought, must be from the starlings. He remembered occasions when they had spattered him as they gathered to nestle in vast numbers in the trees by the park. He doesn't want to go home, obviously. Like me; Tom thought.

"Why today? Why is he always here on Thursdays?' Tom asked. Weekends would be much busier here, he presumed. It came to him as the most innocuous approach towards satisfying his curiosity about who Mike was.

"Gets his money on Thursdays. Benefits."

His neighbour at the counter wiped his goatee beard and looked closely at Tom for the first time. "What line are you in, then?" He was staring at Tom's expensive city jacket.

"Nothing special. Computers, technology," Tom said. He took a swig of his drink. Not for much longer either; he thought, because I might join the barman's son out there, for all I know. He realised he was smiling at the idea. Not because it appealed – the irony of it, perhaps. When you work at something with so much success that it ends up replacing your own job ... or is likely to, anyway ... and knowing that the numbers of lay-offs announced that morning meant last in first out. Which meant he would be one of the employees to go soon.

"Mike wasn't always like this, of course. That's what upsets his dad so much. Would me!" Goatee took hold of Tom's sleeve. Felt the quality of it, no doubt. He pointed at a photograph on the wall behind the bar. "That's his son Mike up there. Not so many years ago, either."

Some pubs show collections of beer mats, postcards, horseshoes and riding bits, if they're country pubs, but this one had panoramic photographs. Illustrating certain specific people, thought Tom, as his gaze travelled along to the one indicated by his neighbour. It showed a group all lined up and looking pleased with themselves.

"That's him," said his neighbour, who was standing up now with his empty glass and leaning over the bar. "The cocky-looking one with the long hair and his arm around the little red-head. Barbara, his wife. I met her once, in better days."

Tom found it hard to reconcile the young man in the photograph with the one ejected from the bar. Success and failure, more than ageing, he judged, might account for that. "Who are they all?' he asked. Tom waved his arm along the length of the prominent, glossy photographic image behind its non-reflective glass.

"The film crew. Camera-man, Mike was. Top man, too." He spoke as though it was all apparent enough, sat back down again on the bar stool and rapped his empty glass on the counter in emphasis.

Tom felt anticipation stirring; his stomach fluttered, and his head was firing questions and possibilities, so he took a calming breath and finished his drink. "I'll get you another when the barman comes back," he said. "What happened, then? How did his son, Mike, get to where he is now? Do you know?"

The man paused, held Tom's look and traced a line with his fingernail through the wet surface of the bar counter. He sniffed, throwing his head back a little. "He's much better just on the booze," he said. "And either way, he hasn't the money for much of anything now." He coughed into his hand and flashed a warning look down to the end of the bar.

Tom took the hint as he saw the barman returning. He extracted a note from his inside jacket pocket and pushed it towards the goatee. 'Here, get in a couple more just for yourself,' he said. "I've got to go."

Tom hurried to the exit and looked up and down the street outside. What if he's gone? How will I find him? But there he was. Standing under the street light, shoulders hunched, and gazing into the gutter. Tom slowed down his approach. A light rain started, so Tom raised the collar of his expensive suit's jacket, realising he no longer had *his* coat. Where did I leave it? –He looked at his watch – two, three hours ago. What have I been doing all that time? He wondered. Mulling over my own disappointments and troubles, I guess.

"Hey, Mike!" He called out loudly when he was a few feet away. The younger man looked up at his name. "It *is* Mike, isn't it? The camera man? Know about your work, Mike. I've got an idea I want to bounce off you. How do you fancy a Chinese or an Italian? There's a good place near here. Could be interesting, man. I'm Tom."

Mike straightened up. He looked alert now and curious; his brow creased as he tried to focus. "Who are you? What do you want?" He moved closer and took Tom's extended hand.

An expert camera man, thought Tom with elation, and not so far gone he can't come back. He's just what I need. He put a hand on Mike's shoulder and steered him further down the street. "There's a good little trattoria down here. Are you hungry, Mike? I am!"

Tom's enthusiasm grew. It's *my* idea and I'll not give it over for the company's use and profits. Not this time. They've made enough out of me. And I know which clients I can approach by the back door. If I can get Mike on board and use his skills, this will be a *done deal* before anyone can even process the development of it, or know anything at all about it.

He thought of that series of TV coffee adverts which had run as a progressive narrative. Telling a story which people wanted to follow. Of how much this bar could change from a Thursday evening with a few sad loners. This is going to be a whole new advertising device, and it's going to make us both some serious money! He opened the door of the restaurant and urged Mike inside.

THE DINNER LADY

The first time I met Stuart, he stuck out his hand in a semblance of greeting and said he didn't do any of that 'kissing business'. It was at an autumnal fête in France on a day of pleasant sunshine, despite the shortening daylight. The venue, a mixed bumpy piece of grass and stones, lay beneath the towering ruins of a castle. Stunned by Stuart's rudeness – they were only 'air' kisses and culturally determined – I stood watching him glance dismissively around the craft and food stalls set up on the mound below the remains of the fortified structure.

I was involved with, but not yet fully part of, a distinct English grouping who were at the event. An intimate crowd of smiling faces, talking fast; asking where you lived, and how far you had got with the renovations of your dilapidated French house. The gathering of people ebbed and flowed between neighbourly talk and the distracting pull of local displays of special cheeses and other dairy products for sale.

Having dismissed me, Stuart turned back to address the English. "None of you should be here. You shouldn't come to live in another country if you haven't got enough capital." His voice was loud and Stuart jabbed a finger at the group. No-one took much notice, shrugging their shoulders and frowning at him before moving away.

Without a response from them, he remembered me. "You staying?" he asked. He splayed his feet on the uneven ground and thrust out his barrel chest. His muscular arms hung forward. A striking figure of masculinity. He breathed with a slight wheeze as he lowered his moon face to talk to me, but did not wait for a reply. "I won't stay long. It isn't much, and I've seen it all before." Then he strode off.

Once he left the scene, others informed me that Stuart hired only local French artisans to work in his own large house by the river and despised those who didn't. Had I seen the house, yet? They emphasised the point that he used expensive labour, which others could not afford. No doubt he was generous, and it gave him considerable status in the small French village, but he did not speak French, and was not well liked. Although I sensed they tolerated him, even if they did not approve of him, the English crowd here on this day liked to talk about Stuart. I learned his hobby was coarse sea fishing, and he indulged it in holidays taken in far-flung parts of the world during the frequent absences of his wife. The latter intrigued me and I probed with a few questions.

His recent display of ill-temper that day was because of a missing driver. He played golf and, somehow, his favourite driving iron had disappeared from the monstrous golf bag, which a caddy had to carry around for him. His current vexation was more likely to be that of his wife. Rosalind, who had gone home to spend time with family in England. Further gossip rumoured that Stuart had disinherited his son, cut him out of his will because he would not give up smoking. They had quarrelled beyond the point of threats and, some said, came to blows about it. Perhaps his wife had gone home in the role of a pacifier?

A man to avoid? It seemed so. Stuart invited

me to celebrate his birthday with friends at a café/bar located under the ruins in a small hamlet a month later. "You pay for your own meal, but Stuart covers the wine," someone whispered. I added my name to the list anyway because I was curious and wanted the company.

The air was chilly as we arrived on that evening. We pushed through the entrance, breathing the wood smoke, eager to get out of the damp mist rising from the river. We sat at one long table, which was already set, and bought drinks from the bar to give us something to do. Smokers disappeared from time to time, returned clasping their arms to themselves, to report how unpleasant it was out there.

More than an hour later, I realised I had twitched my nose at some agreeable spicy aromas and mentioned that to my neighbour, Christine. "I hope the food is going to be good because I'm so hungry I could eat my own shoe leather."

Christine laughed. "Your sandals are far too pretty for that," she said. "Anyway, it's not that late, really." She pointed to the clock above the busy bar on the wall at the far side of the room. She tucked her long skirt closer around her thighs and folded her hands in her lap. I knew little about her; saw her as one of several lonely widows who blended in unnoticed. All the women had to sit on one side of the table opposite the men, and it muddled us up, so that everyone should talk to their closest neighbours. It was a sensible and convivial arrangement.

When the vast, steaming dishes of paella arrived, the noise level had already peaked under the low ceiling of the room, which was an annexe to the older building. The meal was Stuart's choice – he had asked around and come up with something everyone seemed to like – but it was a Spanish dish that the French owners had struggled with. Now it was late in the evening and fuelled by alcoholic appetisers, everyone dived in to satisfy their hunger. For a while, the echoing chatter and laughter faded out, and they opened the wine bottles spaced out down the table.

Replenishment of the paella was called for, and the owners, who were the caterers, soon reappeared with more vast platters of rice and seafood. Finally, the consumption slowed and conversation, perhaps more languid, continued.

At one point, Stuart must have reached the end of one of his stories. A shout rang out, which caused a commotion. "You male chauvinist pig!"

Christine and I looked along the table in confusion to gather, from those nearer the source, what Stuart had said in provocation. We had missed the story, but someone gave us the gist of it. Stuart had been talking about a particular night club in London, and a wealthy old man leaving late with a pretty young woman on his arm. The purpose of the story, according to Stuart's pointed insistence, was that you would never see such a scene in reverse. Wealthy old *men* always got beautiful young women. You never saw a couple where gender and age were the other way round. This comment had triggered the reaction and the appellation of chauvinism to our host.

My meek neighbour, Christine, erupted from her seat. Flushed and roused, she leaned across the long table, drummed her knuckles on it, and in a loud voice demanded Stuart's attention. Her voice carried, and the clutter of cutlery diminished.

"Listen, Stuart. I'll tell you a story. A true one. You could have seen me at that club you're talking about some years ago," she said. Stuart was silenced, perhaps by surprise.

She had been between marriages, Christine told us, and an old girlfriend, knowing Christine loved to dance, had arranged a night out on the tiles. Buoyed by some alcohol, but to a much greater degree by the dancing, Christine had returned to their table to rest during an interval. It was at that moment a very smart, 'drop-dead gorgeous' young man had approached the two women. He insisted on dancing with Christine. As they danced, he confessed, trembling, that he knew her! As a schoolboy, she had had an important role in his life. He remembered her as his dinner lady and had recognised her that night at the club. He told her he had fantasised about her while a schoolboy, and ever since.

By the end of that evening in the nightclub, she had agreed to leave with him and to fulfil his dreams. They went to his luxurious flat and had a wonderful, passionate weekend together, which she would never forget. He still sent her red roses every year to remember that time.

Christine had been glaring at Stuart throughout the tale. "So, you see, there are times when a wealthy, handsome young man leaves a nightclub with his arms wrapped around an older woman!"

Whoops of delight and applause broke out. Stuart sat back wordlessly, but his wife seized the moment and led us to raise our glasses to toast him on his birthday. It calmed down after that.

For me, Christine became 'the lady with the stories'. We met from time to time, but she was not happy in a new relationship in France because her partner's family disliked them living together. He was weak and let his visiting family drive the couple apart.

As for Stuart; not long after that night, they diagnosed his wife with the pernicious cancer that killed her. She never knew, until the very last, that it was terminal. Stuart had always protected her from that. It was at this time and later that I witnessed such a different side to the man.

In the years following her death, we still continued an acquaintance with Stuart and wondered what would happen to him.

He did not sell the house in France, nor return to England, but he continued to take extensive holidays abroad in exotic locations where he could fish – his primary aim and major hobby. Despite much surgery, to replace joints weakened by injuries sustained during his career in the Metropolitan police, his health was further undermined. The bitter winters in that part of France – so vicious that you did not quite believe in the summer's return with its infernos – suited him less and less.

He could not live in the French house because of the memories. Yet, he confided to me; it drew him back, as he tried to find Rosalind again. Once, he spent a long period in Thailand and people thought he would return to France with a beautiful young woman in his life. He was wealthy, and it would have been easy. He never did. Somehow, I knew that he never would.

THE FISHING BOAT

She didn't notice it at first, part of the scenery, although an incongruous part. Such an old and dilapidated fishing boat; a wreck, jammed up on the shoreline. When the real focal point was the prestigious fan-shaped mooring of yachts, which dominated the scene of the inner harbour.

The boat was just there, natural, organic. Not like a mass of rotting driftwood, or some unsightly debris might be. Battered but colourful. The torn hull streaked with green, yellow and red; the remnants of a once painted pattern. Perhaps because of some sort of impact, the tilted wheelhouse had slid off the vertical, but the box structure on the deck, where the catch of fish funnelled down into the hold, was still intact and gave evidence of the working purpose of the vessel.

Her gaze moved across the deep blue of the water down into the reflections of the old submarine pens across the other side of the inner harbour. A deep blue sea matched by an almost cloudless sky. She stood listening to the tinkling distraction of a soft breeze through the stays on the masts of the yachts, rising against the intermittent gulls' harsh squawking.

Of course, this wasn't the height of the season and the weather would change, make it less picturesque. They had bought the timeshare for the small apartment for holidays in the early summer – as the last big splurge of a retirement dividend. It would all look quite different in a wintry gale, she thought. A wintry gale would make me less enamoured of it.

"Come on Maggie. What are you doing? Let's find some lunch." He joined her on the balcony and put his arm around her.

"What do you think happened to the fishing boat?" she asked. She leaned over the balcony and pointed to it.

"Who knows? Probably just abandoned because it wasn't seaworthy any more.

It's surprising no-one has removed it. Bit of an eyesore in a place like this."

Her French was good enough to do more than ask for directions and question items on a menu. She could make small talk and enjoyed doing so. Perhaps she would find someone to ask about the boat? She breathed in, tasting salt on her tongue, as they strolled along in the sunshine, holding hands, and she steered him towards the boat, wanting a closer look.

Peter indulged her whim, but he could see nothing remarkable in the wreck. Instead, he stood with his face turned up, welcoming the warmth of the sun, and regardless of the uncomfortable glare. She let her imagination wander. Her gaze drifted to an old man, sprightly and smart in appearance, crossing the junction of a side road and coming towards them. He looked so obviously French. As he approached, he slowed down as if inviting a greeting. She mused he was a local, taking a stroll before his lunch.

"Bonjour, Monsieur. Quel beau matin!"

She knew that a comment on the weather was

just as good an introduction, whether you were in France or England, and he seemed to want one.

He replied in a similar fashion. On an impulse, she pointed to the boat and asked him if he knew anything about it. He said it had been there for a long time. Despite the submarine pens opposite, which could lead her astray, the boat did not date from as far back as the last century; he advised her. He was making the reference, no doubt, because she was English, and the connection with wartime Europe would come to mind. They exchanged a few more words on the beauty of the location, and he wished them a happy holiday.

Later, at the nearby restaurant where they ate a delicious meal from a fresh catch, she tried again to find out about the boat from some residents at an adjacent table. They apologised because, although French, they were newcomers, but asked a waiter for her. Again, she drew a blank.

Maggie gave up after that. She grew used to the sight of the boat from the balcony of the apartment. It became an integral part of the view.

****

They had many holiday photographs of the apartment with the wonderful view. Looking through them always reminded her of the boat and its history. So when they returned the following year, she looked for it immediately, as usual on their arrival. But it was gone.

At first, she thought it must have moved to a different place where it had got stuck on the land rather than moored in the shallows. Tides vary and can do that, she told herself. She checked all along the frontage of that part of the harbour. How could it have moved so far away and out of view? Could she have made a mistake about its position? She kept peering down from the balcony with a growing sense of loss.

"The local authority – *commune*, or whatever it is – must have moved it, after all." Peter said.

She supposed they found out who had beached it there, who had owned it and abandoned it. Some people would think it an eyesore. It would not please them and there could have been complaints; the resort prided itself on the beauty of the view.

Peter suggested its removal had taken place for some shrewd developer. A business man contemplating that little piece of shoreline. But she refused to believe in such a desecration.

Maggie could not let the matter rest. Could they have taken it somewhere else? She disliked the idea that it would remain a mystery because, if no-one knew how and when it arrived, why should anyone have noticed its departure? She wondered if a winter squall had swept it away further out into the open sea and broken it up so that it sank. The view seemed incomplete now. She missed the boat. Its absence gave her a disquieting feeling of the loss of something important.

One morning, taking breakfast on the balcony, sipping coffee and spreading a croissant with a tart, tangy jam, she watched men walking along the line of the harbour beneath the block of apartments. Their talk was loud, and they gesticulated all the time. One looked middle-aged and appeared to supervise the others, another carried a bag of tools, and a third heaved a short, stout plinth. They approached the area where the boat had been. The middle-aged one stood still for a long time, looking out across the harbour and turning to gaze out to sea.

After breakfast, Maggie and Peter left the apartment building for a morning stroll. The men were no longer in view, but she thought they might still be there somewhere beside the harbour, if she was quick.

She pulled at Peter's elbow, making him red faced and annoyed by her urge to hurry. As they left the building, she could not hold back from running across the street and leaving him behind. Even the man who had delayed to gaze across the harbour had gone. Only an upright plinth remained for her inspection. It was neither a recognisable traffic sign nor a tourist indicator of nearby attractions. Perhaps they had not finished it yet? Peter caught up and could not understand her interest or her deep sense of connection.

Afterwards, she felt as if she were waiting for something to happen and only hoped the holiday would not be over before she found out what it was. The days flew past in the usual lazy way of enjoyment and jumbled memories. They returned to favourite restaurants from the previous year, took part in a maritime festival, and explored further along the coast.

Finally, she saw the middle-aged man once again. She recognised him both by his position there on the shoreline, by the plinth, and in the stillness of his stance. It was late in the afternoon, when the sun had dipped and the balcony was in shadow, cooling by the minute.

She ran past Peter in the sitting room, reading a brochure. "I won't be a minute, darling. Just carry on," she said.

Maggie did not wait for the lift. She was already planning what she might say to him. Of course, he must be French. Her approach was not too difficult. Perhaps he read the earnestness of her expression and accepted, even approved, of the formality of her greeting.

His name was Michel. They shook hands. She explained her interest in the boat, which had always been there when they came on holiday, and had disappeared. He relaxed, abandoning his limited English.

He told her the boat had belonged to his father. A lobster fisherman who had drowned at sea. The empty boat had drifted into the harbour and came to rest there on the shoreline. Maggie paused and posed her intrusive questions about the tragedy with great care. Wanting to know, but not to offend, and she was aware of the language barrier and how easy it was to say the wrong thing. How long ago had it happened? Had there been a storm? His answers were sparse in detail, acknowledging again the accident at sea.

Michel had known for a long time that the boat had to be removed. Though, as far as he could see, its presence had done no harm. But officialdom had caught up with him. He had not felt able to do anything about the boat until now because it was all too painful, and he had needed more time.

She guessed about the plinth and pointed to it to distract him. It was a memorial, which he had sought and had gained permission to install as a plinth there. As well as a plaque, which had also gained approval. It was, if you like, he suggested with a smile, part of the terms of his agreement to remove the boat.

It pleased Maggie to know his father would be remembered. But she asked if it was not sad for him to think of the boat towed away and broken up. She mentioned that her own father had taken to sailing in his retirement. Although now he could remember nothing of those days. Michel looked troubled. My father was spared that, he acknowledged, he was not in his prime, but not in decline either. She wondered if her own sense of loss was the connection that first drew her to the fate of the boat. She did not tell Michel that *her* father could not even remember who she was before they left, this time, for their holiday.

"Oh, no! I will not allow the boat to be broken up," Michel said. "It's an old boat, part of an era, and I intend to restore it. Then I will take her out to sea again, which will be a reminder of when I was a boy with him."

Michel took her hand in an almost courtly farewell. "Come back and you will see her, I promise. I will show her to you."

You have to take time and select them; she thought. Those memories that will linger…

UNWELCOME ENCOUNTERS

Julie had been worrying since the afternoon tea break. When she ambled, distracted, into the kitchenette, she found only a couple of people slumped in the easy chairs lined against the back wall, and both of them looked morose. No-one spoke, which made her feel worse. While she was at her desk, taking the calls and whipping through the information screens, she did not think about it. Well, the image was always on the periphery, but banished. That was the difference.

She remained standing, cupping the milky coffee from the machine and sipping it, and gazed out of the window to the rooftops beyond. It had stopped raining, yet the view remained dismal. A quick, habitual glance at the ceiling, up into the corners, and her shoulders sank down enough to force them to relax. She did not want to go home, and nothing would change that.

"What's up with you, then?" Jonathan stood

in her path when she returned to her work station. At least he bothered to notice, to look at her, weighing up her expression and reacting to it. "Oh, review day tomorrow – sorry,"

Julie flushed. "Not that," she said, and turned away, veering off at an angle to hurry the return to her office place. She had no wish to enlighten him. It was true, too. She had no fears at the prospect of the routine work assessment. In fact, the line manager had already told her she was up for a bonus.

Speedy, unflappable, and with all the knowledge she needs at her fingertips. Those were the exact words. Remembering them, Julie's lips curved in a slow smile. By the time she reached her desk, she was almost at ease once more. Work helped.

All too soon, the afternoon session of her shift ended. Her heart pounded at the sudden eruption of chatter, movement; people pushing back their ergonomic work chairs, curling up their identity cards hanging on the straps around their necks, and tossed them into desk drawers. They rushed to the glass exit doors and the staff cloakrooms.

After the afternoon's calming atmosphere of rhythmic clicks on keyboards, soft mutterings into headpieces, and the light swish of seats as the occupants crossed and re-crossed stiff limbs, the noise of departure had reached such a startling crescendo she felt dizzy.

She only just caught the usual bus home, having avoided a long wait for the next one, which was the usual reason. Of course, she had not hurried in the walk home which followed the bus journey. Delaying tactics. She paused at a stretch of shop windows, glanced at the parish notice board, and spoke a few words to a passing woman with an adorable *Westie* – Julie liked dogs. The animal responded well to her caresses, and the owner looked on with a broad grin. To admire a pet was to compliment the owner, or so it always seemed.

In the end, though, she had to climb the staircase to her floor and enter her flat. Turning the front door key, she paused a moment after slipping inside, then pulled it closed behind her and took a casual stroll down the hallway. At first, Julie held her head high, but it soon drooped. A wary investigation followed, in which she was on tip-toes.

Why creep about? She admonished herself. *What good will that do?*

That night, to avoid it she dragged a clean duvet out of the airing cupboard and slept on the sofa instead of in her bed. She left the curtains wide open and took solace from the velvety night sky lit by a street lamp and the unusual quantity of stars to dream about. Mesmeric.

Julie drifted off to sleep and woke in good time for a quick breakfast of instant porridge before leaving for work the next day.

*****

It was during the review of her employment that she inexplicably went to pieces. Tearful, her shoulders shaking, she accepted a glass of water, grateful it was only half-full, as her hands were shaking so much.

"Whatever happens here and now, you have attained another promotion, Julie. No question," said Danielle. She stooped over Julie and patted her shoulder twice, before withdrawing as if she thought she might have offended her colleague with the personal contact.

Danielle dropped the temporary tool to the floor and kicked it under her desk. "Sorry about that. A reminder, of course ….I should have noticed it was there."

Out of sight and out of mind, thank goodness for that. Julie grabbed another tissue from the box. Inoffensive items in themselves, she thought. Everyday things which Danielle had put to such a strange purpose of removal. It almost made her laugh, though she recognised it as the onset of hysterics. Aware that the wide-open window blasted fresh, cold air, Julie stood up, breathed in several times, and straightened her back. Then she closed the window and Danielle looked relieved, smiling and waving her back into a chair. Danielle had done the deed, and there was no need to expose her to the chill of cold air any longer, so Julie closed the window.

"Thank you. You've been so kind," Julie said. She forced back tears and regained her self-control.

"I'm going to arrange an appointment for you with our Welfare Officer," Danielle said. She raised her eyebrows in mute enquiry, and reached for the phone, after Julie had nodded her assent.

There was a wide difference between their ages; Julie thought. I could be Danielle's mother. You never know about people. I always felt awkward taking orders from Danielle. Not as if they were orders, because she has a gentle way with her. Sometimes I think she is fragile underneath. Julie remembered the first time she had seen Danielle's boyfriend. He did not appeal because on that occasion, when he came into the office to collect her, he had seemed abrupt, even harsh, with no sense of intimacy between them. Yet, the rumour was that they were close and thinking of moving in together.

With her increased status, not forgetting the incremental boosts in her salary, Julie's work situation changed over the next months and also her social life. The two women enjoyed each other's company outside of work, finding what they had in common.

One weekend, while waiting for their order at the local bistro, Julie discussed her progress with Danielle. The Welfare Officer, a sensible and knowledgeable woman, had organised several sessions of therapy, including desensitisation. This had helped and, although their problems were not the same, understanding each other's fears had blossomed into a solid friendship between Julie and her boss, Danielle. They had laughed about the age gap between them and their unique status and relationship in the office.

"Did you know that Britain has the biggest house spiders in Europe?" Julie asked.

"Yes, you've already told me that," said Danielle. The sudden change of subject did not surprise her, having flinched as the waitress touched her hand on her return with the cake plate. "I didn't do too badly there, did I, Julie? Did you notice?"

"Brilliant," said Julie. "Let's raise a toast to ourselves with our coffee. It was the way they often ended their visit to the bistro. They clinked cups and spoke the words. "To the *arachnophobia! And the haphephobic!*

*Arachnophobia – fear of spiders

*Haphephobic - fear of touch

THE ATTIC

George climbed the ladder up to the attic and sneezed so hard he almost lost his footing. Regaining stability, he raised his head 'above the parapet', as he liked to think of it, and edged his way onto the safety of the dusty wooden boards of the floor. "Not much left". He coughed because of the dust. The low space in the eaves needed care and this time he would make sure he did not hit his head on that wretched beam. As it was, he had to bend, even crouch down in places, whenever he came up here. And there had been a lot of trips up here to the attic, which was why all this dust was disturbed and had got right up his nose.

Downsizing was sensible now. Their daughter Tanya was well-established in her own flat in the business centre of the town; George thought. But the upheaval of their own move seemed relentless. Tanya had given up a lot of her precious time though, and it pleased them to see her busy and enthusiastic in her career; independent and making her own way in life.

Perhaps, when this was all over, he and Lena

could dip into the extra capital from the down-sizing and take a luxury holiday. Just the two of them. Do something adventurous – white water kayaking came to mind – but he dismissed it with a smile and a shrug. Water sports were not at all his wife, Lena's style. He spotted and manoeuvred the case he had to retrieve. He wondered what exactly his wife's style was now.

Tanya had taken several pieces off them – good, solid furniture, which was too large for the bijou, riverside cottage her parents were moving into. Other old and odd things, too. But dusting off the top of the wooden framed box he had picked up, it puzzled him why their daughter would want this. It could be valuable, he supposed. Was it considered retro and fashionable now?

George placed it with care at the top of the trapdoor, eased himself back onto the platform of the ladder, and descended with caution. He took it straight to the car and, loaded once more, drove to his new home.

The riverside cottage had two notable advantages over their old family home. Though the living space was tiny, there was a double-sized garage (and they only had one car) and also a workshop – ramshackle, but with potential. George unloaded what he hoped were the last items from the car. He had destined the few remaining bits and pieces in the attic for the skip and, afterwards for the council 'tip'.

He stood looking down the river bank into the distance, listening to the water' gentle flow and watching the play of light on the trees producing the rippling reflections. When he sorted out that hearing test, in future he might even hear the birdsong. Perhaps that workshop could become a boathouse one day. Then he could enjoy the river, and so would Lena. It would make all the upheaval worthwhile. They hadn't got as far as discussing any future projects yet; it felt as though selling one home and buying another had drained away all their energy.

George remembered Lena would be late home. It had been his turn to take some leave, and she was still working flat out. I am not incompetent in the kitchen; he reminded himself and wanted something to prepare for a hot and tasty evening meal. He would look in the fridge and the cupboards to see what Lena had left in there. And find a bottle of wine to go with it. They had located no convenience store as yet, and he did not want to set off again for the town.

A week later, George and Lena felt settled in. They ate dinner with the curtains left open for as long as possible *every* evening, enjoying the view of the river, the colourful craft and the people on them, and the sheer variety of water and skyscape images as Spring advanced. It was all novel, and they were delighted with the change in their lives resulting from the new environment. Tanya was due for Sunday lunch and Lena was singing in the kitchen. George turned up the music and gave her a twirl until she was flushed and laughing. Perhaps they would get back into dancing as well. George brought her to a halt and clasped her to him when he heard the bell. He walked through to let Tanya in, while Lena put the fruit pie in the oven.

"Oh, darling, you shouldn't have bothered with all that," said Lena. She took the flowers and chocolates from her daughter and put them on the worktop with a broad smile. "I'll get fat on these!"

"Serve you right," said Tanya. "Remember all those gorgeous puddings you used to force on me? Can I give you a hand, mum?"

"Yes. Thank you. No, wait a minute. As you've brought gifts … George, get that surprise for Tanya, will you? It's time she had it. Lots of memories there, darling." Lena turned back to her daughter and gathered her close in a hug.

George did as he was bid. *Lots of memories? What on earth did Lena mean?* He struggled across from the garage with the 'memento'. It was not very heavy, just awkward, and he wanted the glass to remain intact. Luckily, he had not cracked it yet, and today would be just the wrong moment for his luck to run out. That description surprised him, though. Perhaps his daughter had a new hobby or was developing a rare skill. A dying skill? That could be it! And there would be money in that, too. *Our clever girl!*

When he returned, Tanya and Lena were sipping wine and had their heads together. There was a rumour, he understood, that Tanya had a new boyfriend and was very keen on him. *Women's talk, then.* George heaved the glass case onto the worktop. "Do you want me to give it to her, or will you? Anyway, here it is, sweetie."

At first, no answer came. Then Lena screamed. It was short, but not sweet.

"Whaaa what?" said Tanya. "What on earth is that?"

Bemused, George looked at them and babbled. "Well, it *is* old. Your mum said it would remind you of your childhood. Things that have been around while you were young and growing up. And this thing must have been around a long …. " His explanation faltered.

"George!"

He could not ignore Lena's tone, and he approached her with a frown on his face and eyes blinking in confusion and fearful anticipation. "I said get Tanya's old box. The one in the attic which I had packed with such love; school things, mother's day cards she made me and old toys and clothes …" Lena looked tearful now. Tanya seemed fixated on the glass case. She was struggling, too.

George sat down heavily on the sofa and clasped his head in his hands. He looked at the two women and in desperation took a deep breath before he said, "The old *fox* in the attic, Lena. I thought you meant this stuffed *fox* in the attic." He pointed to the dried out rather mangy looking animal, which dated back to Victoria's reign.

"And where, George, is her *box* in the attic? The box full of our daughter's childhood memories?" asked Lena. There was something icy in her look.

"Er …." George realised it served no purpose to delay the punch line.

"That box, I have to think, was in the skip

outside our house, then. Nothing to distinguish it, my dear. Honest. But, by now, I imagine, I'm afraid, it is at our local tip. Sorry!"

THE BIG THREE O

"Greg! Sorry, but I'm ever so busy right now," said Jenny. She held the door half open and sighed.
"That's what you always say. Well, nearly always," said Greg. He pushed the door wide and took two steps forward before halting in her hallway. "Can I come in?"
"You already are. What's that you've got behind your back?" Jenny had glimpsed a flash of colour.
"Make me a coffee and I'll show you."
Jenny led the way into the kitchen. She had already put the kettle on and, as she turned to take another mug out of the cupboard, she glanced with weariness at the pile of assignments on the table.
"If I could just get those finished," she said, pointing to the heap of papers. "Then I might actually get a bit of peace this half-term."
She spooned coffee into the machine.
Although how I ended up with that lethargic lot, as my group, I will never know. Plagiarised ideas and paragraphs copied straight from sample texts. They will be trying

to find and use AI essays soon.

She turned back to look at Greg, who was waiting, standing as if called to strict attention, with one arm still behind his back, and a comic grimace on his face. He bowed, revealing the tail end of a tantalising piece of cellophane and ribbons, and then thrust the bouquet towards her.

"Happy birthday!"
"You remembered." Jenny smiled for the first time that morning and took the flowers from him. "They're lovely. Do they have any scent?"
"I hope so. Open them up and find out."
She unwound the ribbon and slipped scissors through the cellophane. Putting her nose right into the mass of red blooms, she took a deep breath. "That really is gorgeous: all musky. Thank you, Greg. You can have some coffee in a few minutes. I'll get the milk. And I must put these in water straight away."
Jenny had to stretch up to reach the vase and was flexing her fingertips around the base of the crystal-glass on the top of a cupboard. Greg promptly stepped up behind her, rescued the vase, lifting it over her head, and brushed

a kiss against her neck. It made her giggle, and she gave him a hug with the vase clutched between them.

As she arranged the blooms, Jenny counted them. "Are there thirty stems, by any chance?"

"Of course. And that's what all this is about, isn't it?" Greg said to her back. Jenny remained silent, and he saw her stiffen her shoulders. Had he done the wrong thing? "All this tremendous work ethic you've developed all of a sudden. You were never that devoted to your career, as far as I am aware, so I was beginning to wonder where it was all coming from," he said.

"Some of us have to work hard to earn a living." Jenny turned round to face him now as her cheeks reddened. She leaned back against the worktop with her arms crossed across her chest. "If you had had to climb the slippery pole, from the background of a family of six kids, with never a penny between us, you might understand."

Greg poured milk into his coffee. His hair flopped over his brow and Jenny restrained a smile at his boyish appearance. They were of much the same age and he was attractive. Not yet her boyfriend, but promising.

"I suppose you are off again to do some DIY work in France next week?" she asked. "Lucky, for some, to have a holiday home abroad."

Greg put down his mug. "Don't be so critical, Jen; you know the cottage is nothing much, and I've worked hard on it. This isn't *really,* you. Look, I've booked dinner for tonight at a new restaurant, which I have already tried – I know how fussy you are – and it has a good range of vegetarian dishes regularly on the menu. You can wear a nice frock, and feel special. Which you are."

He gave her an appraising and appreciative look from head to foot. Jenny's immediate response was to lift her chin and draw in her waist.

"That low-necked one with the little straps would look quite something, as I recall," said Greg.

"If I can still get into it, that is."

"Of course, you can. It's only another year, Jen. Just one more day, really. Yesterday you were twenty-nine, and today you are thirty. Just one day."

Jenny placed the arrangement of flowers on the table and stepped back to admire them.

"As to the house, the renovation work is all

but finished. It's basic but comfortable now. You could come with me next week and spend half-term there," he ventured. "You deserve a proper break and … I can't think of anyone else I would rather share it with."

"Yes, perhaps we could talk about it over dinner?" The prospect appealed to Jenny.

"I'll leave you in peace then for now. So you can get on with … whatever that pile is. For marking, I would guess." Greg stood up and tucked the bar stool under the breakfast bar.

"Don't I even get a kiss before I go?"

"The flowers are lovely. Thank you, Greg."

She gave him a kiss, and he hugged her close. Lifting her up to make her laugh.

After he had gone, Jenny gathered up the students' papers and clasped them to her chest. She felt her heart beating faster, with more warmth than she had wanted to acknowledge. There was still time to join him in his usual ferry crossing to France.

Her aim had always been for stability and a career was the way to make sure of that. But it did not mean that you had to 'go it alone' all the time. Her mood lifted.

I'll just finish the grades on these assignments; she thought. There must be at least a few of them that are worthy of a straight A. Encouragement can work wonders. Then I'll see if I can find that dress Greg mentioned. I think I know the one.

IT'S CHRISTMAS, SO HAVE ANOTHER BEER!

Sarah watched as her brother, John, took a second big gulp from the glass. "This tastes peculiar," he said.
"Oh, get that one down your throat, and I'll pour you another," said Sarah.
John stretched out his long legs as far as he could in the confined space of the sitting room, which seemed even more crowded with the addition of the Christmas tree. He held the glass up before him. "What is it, anyway? Where did you get it from?"
"We did a mini booze-cruise a couple of months ago."
Sarah's mind was elsewhere as she checked the room. Mum looks happy, even if it is a cramped room in here; she thought.
John hunched his shoulders down and nestled further into the armchair. "That big shopping place in Calais? Foreign rubbish, then. You

cheapskate!"

Sarah curled the habitual strand of mouse-brown hair around one finger as she listened for the doorbell. "No, we went into Calais itself. Had some lunch, and then we went to a supermarket there – you get a better range of wines than on the booze cruise crossings. Anyway, the lager *you* drink is 'foreign': it's not made in Britain."

"Perhaps I should change over to some superior wine, then?"

Sarah looked at the shirt stretched and clinging to her brother's midriff. "Stick with the beer. You're a beer man, brother dear, as your belly proves!"

John laughed and eased himself upright.

Sarah bustled into the kitchen to get another beer from the fridge. They were ice cold, as she knew he liked them. The only trouble with John was that he always had so many on these family occasions, and then he often got rude and started shouting, and spoiled it for Mum. But perhaps not today, she hoped.

She glanced around the sitting room again, obsessed with the lack of space. Since their mother's widowhood, she had arranged a relaxed family gathering just prior to Christmas. Everyone contributed something towards it, turning up with an offering of food or drink.

The bell rang, and she edged her way through the maze of legs and side-tables to open the front door. "So glad you made it. You're the last ones … last but not least." Her sister Judith with husband David and their little girl stepped inside. "That's a pretty party frock, Katie." Sarah picked her up and gave her a hug.

Judith took the lid off the tin she held and revealed, with a flourish, an elaborate cake decorated in red, gold and silver – the traditional Christmas colours. "Wow! Love the icing," said Sarah.

"It was fun doing it." Judith said and put the cake down on the breakfast table in the kitchen. The others trooped back into the narrow hallway to hang up their coats. "It's pelting down out there. Hope we haven't put muddy, wet prints all over your carpet," she said and kicked off her shoes. "New, isn't it?"

"The carpet? No, of course not. Not just before Christmas. It's an expensive time, isn't it?" She watched Katie run past her mother, glance at the base of the tree, and then head straight to the sofa where her grandmother was sitting with her legs up. Katie snuggled up under granny's arm, nestling close, and pulled a twist of her hair into her mouth and sucked it.

I wonder if I did that, too, at her age; Sarah thought. As she pulled Katie in even closer, she heard her mother mutter, "If they all bicker later, I'll let it all roll over me, as usual. They mean well, my little pet. You're never a problem, are you?"

Peering at the weather through the clouded glass, Sarah agreed it was miserable outside; rain sleeting down the pane like a plastic waterfall and the light already going. She opened the small top window for some air. John caught her eye, raised his empty glass, and moved out of his chair.

"Coming John, I'll get it!" she called. His cheeks were already red, but she thought it was just the heat in the crowded room. Sarah assessed his appearance. She had not seen him for a long time and noticed he had put on a lot of weight. She still thought he was an attractive-looking man: thick, wavy, black hair, not receding yet, and heavy-lashed brown eyes. I wish he could find another woman; she thought. That might stop the drinking.

Peter wanted to make a little welcoming

speech. Sarah rapped a spoon on a wine glass and a hush spread around the room.

"Don't worry, I won't go on for too long," said her husband and gave his usual throaty laugh.

"That'll be the first time, then!" said Judith. The others ignored her.

It was John, as usual, who was the last to leave after draining yet another beer. Sarah saw him out of the door. Still, there was nothing for him to go home to, she thought, with a pang of sympathy. He had been amiable throughout; no sign of the irritability drifting into confrontation; the slide into arguments that often marked family occasions. It had been a successful and festive event.

*****

It was lunchtime the following day, when John appeared again on Sarah's doorstep. She took a step back in surprise before beckoning him into the hallway. "I have just put the kettle on, John. I think sometimes you men can smell there is tea."

John stooped to peck at her cheek. "I'll join you in a cuppa," he said. "You are my favourite Sis, you know that, don't you?"

Sarah led the way into her kitchen, made tea, and put the biscuit barrel on the table. John was scrolling through messages on his smart phone. A new expensive one, of which he was very proud. "What are you doing round here on a workday, anyway?" she interrupted him.
"I'm in my lunch break, if you don't mind, Sarah."
"I didn't mean anything," she said. "You're always welcome here."
John tucked the phone away in a pocket. "I just wanted to come and tell you what happened last night. Quite a story! I have to tell it to someone." He rolled his big brown eyes in a mysterious fashion.
Sarah smiled at his daft expression. "Don't tell me you have found the love of your life."
John lowered his head to take a sip of tea. "No, not that."
"Well?" Sarah asked and pushed the biscuits towards him.
"You know how wet it was when I left yesterday? But I had a big, black brolly, you saw that?" Sarah nodded. "I only brought the car to your place because it was raining so hard, but I never intended to drive it home! It's only a ten-minute walk, and I had the brolly for that."

Sarah's eyes widened in horror. "I should hope not. I would have phoned a cab if I thought you were going to drive."

"Trouble was, I had to stop and get something out of the car. Well, I slipped on the kerb – it was teeming down out there. But I never intended to *drive*," he emphasised, tapping his fingers hard on the table.

"Of course not. You're not a fool, John, and you had had a few. Not that I had been counting."

"I got in the car and leaned over to get my job sheet out of the glove compartment. An old girl I needed to phone first thing, and the part I ordered for her hadn't arrived, so there was no point in going there until later this week. But she was expecting me early, so I had to let her know. I needed her phone number, you see, and that was on the job sheet."

Sarah picked up her mug of tea and took a mouthful. John will tell this in his own way; she thought.

"I was just looking at the bit of paper. Found the number. Then there was a tap on the window. Driver's side, of course. I looked up and, well, it was pouring down, but there was this copper standing there and another one behind him. She was a woman, though."

"Don't tell me. They had seen you slip on the kerb and thought you were drunk!"

"Exactly right, Sis. Well. I had a skin-full, too, at your place. That's true enough. But I would not drive. I am not that daft, am I? You just said as much."

"So, what happened?"

"Showed them all my papers. No problem there. He had put his nose in the car window and had a good sniff at the beginning, the copper, and could smell the booze. You couldn't miss it. Not beer. But I hadn't even put my keys in the ignition. I told them I had no intention of driving!" John slammed his tea mug down on the table. "Listen to this. Apparently, you can be drunk in charge of a car. Drunk in charge of a car, even if you aren't driving. Just sitting in it!" John was almost shouting now.

"Did they breathalyse you, then?"

"Yes, of course they did. But that was the funniest thing …." He looked at her and she saw his puzzlement and the deep creases of his frown.

"Go on. What then?"

"No problem. Negative! I don't think they could believe it. I couldn't believe it you know," said John. His mouth gaped and his eyes widened in amazement. "Do you know they even talked me into having a second one? Negative! I tell you, Sarah, cats have nine lives, they say, but I think that must be my ninth. Can you imagine what would have happened to the business if I had lost my licence? *And* I wasn't even driving the car."

Sarah got up and put a little more hot water into the teapot. She had to turn away so he could not see her broad smile. When he had calmed down, she would tell him what she had done.

"Another cup, John? There is more in the pot."

John was not a fool and he would never drink and drive; Sarah thought. He will be even more careful now. He might even change his drinking habits.

She tapped the box full of empty bottles with her foot and pushed it further into the corner by the sink. She took a sly look at all John's beer bottles clustered together in the centre.

141

When he got the chance to pour out a beer for himself from my fridge yesterday, thank goodness, that John had no clue those two words on the bottles –*'sans alcool'* – meant non-alcoholic.

FLEETING SHADES

She was here today, warming her hands against the stove that wasn't there. Such a sweet, chubby, cherubic face with rose-pink lips. As she swung the thick trailing plait of her hair, the sun through the glass of the long windows encapsulated her head in a halo. She bore a look and stance of such innocence that I gasped, as if a shard had pierced my chest as I sucked my breath inward. I knew there was something tragic about her. An event which should never have happened.
I watched her. Outside in the pure, crystalline frost of an early morning, I saw the young girl playing. I heard her little boots crunching and looked out of the classroom into the gravel yard. Worn and scruffy those boots, but at least she was shod and did not look cold in her pinafore over the shabby dress. She laughed and her breath danced in the chilly air. I watched her call out to nameless others, waving her arms. Her cheeks bloomed red before she was gone.
We had bought the schoolhouse on an impulse in the last few dark days before Christmas the

previous year. The price was cheap and the whole aspect of the building attracted me. My husband, Nick, was not so sure, at first. The owner, who lived somewhere in Paris, had renewed the roof; as so many French did, knowing the English always studied the condition of a roof. This one had immaculate pink tiles reflected in a shaft of afternoon sunlight. It was the one aspect which pleased Nick on the day we first saw the building.

Of course I loved it, I told him, ignoring the size of the building, its antiquated facilities, the mass of overgrown brambles which dwarfed the potential of the fruit trees and the shrubs. I even described the row of child-size outdoor urinals, and lavatories without doors with low, rusting, unseated toilet bowls – the whole almost ruined by the elements – as 'wonderful and evocative of the period'.

The English were snapping up properties everywhere, but no-one else wanted an abandoned school like this; lived in long ago by a handful of nuns in a defunct religious teaching order, and in an isolated village, which boasted one diminutive cafe/bar and a garage with a retired mechanic as its only facilities.

It was early the following year, long before

the start of spring, that I saw her again. After a dedicated group of friends returned home, having helped us to complete a renovation of some of the interior. The building was comfortable now and felt like a holiday home, even though an over large one.

"You might not have paid much for it, but I bet it drains money!" our friend and indefatigable helper, Michael, said. He had a property in Brittany, but on a much smaller scale. He knew technical expressions for building and construction, which had proved invaluable.

On that morning, the floral smell of cleaning fluid hung in the air over the fresh grouting of slabs of floor tiles. It felt empty with our friends just departed, and even the echoes in the vast space of the high-ceilinged *ballroom* were tinged with melancholy. I missed the noise and the busyness of them all.

The schoolroom, a large rectangle with one whole side of ceiling to floor glass windows, provided immediate access to the school yard through three evenly interspersed doors. It was warm now because of the row of radiators. We had installed a new central heating system and an expensive boiler to run it. We called it the *ballroom* and knew that we could not afford to run the heating for long and we wasted it in the vast space we did not yet use.

*****

The sight of the child made me want to know about the building's history. I learned a few scraps during a convenient convivial evening with a group of old 'boys', sitting in proximity within the cafe/bar. Nick and I joined the celebration of a man turning 90 by buying some local Pineau and toasting him with the others. I spoke some French, and that helped.

Mention of the figure of the child, which I had seen twice now, did not bring forth the expected averted gazes or amused smiles. They even told me her name: Bernadette. She was a pupil at the school, in the early part of the previous century, who had died violently and was young. The tale was full of rumour and contradiction, which induced both red-faced annoyance and indignation amongst some in the group of locals. Disputatious because it was her father who had accidentally killed his own child. Did he get his just deserts? He had a tragic end because they executed him for the killing, whether or not warranted. Details they gave included a reference to a report of the father, shackled in a cart, taken to the nearest town for judgement.

In these days, the village had only a visiting priest, not in residence, who presided over irregular services in the fine church, but he had also shown interest in the infamous story when he first said Mass for them. They had remembered this and suggested I should consult him. I resolved to do so as soon as possible because we never stayed for more than a few weeks at a time.

Meanwhile, Bernadette was not alone in her ephemeral appearances, although Nick never witnessed them, and I soon avoided even mentioning them. The evening with the locals at the bar gave some credence to my awareness of the 'presences', as they called them, and I was grateful for that.

"You always were a bit … 'fey'," Nick eventually said. "There's that superstitious idea about the seventh child of the seventh child, which you are, Carol. I suppose there could be something in it. Your mother always believed it."

At the beginning of May that year, we had returned to the house for work on the garden:

to tidy the small orchard at the rear of the building and for the laying of a patio to run along the rear wall. This we intended to manage ourselves.

This time we had arrived on a cold first of May, when French neighbours, by tradition, exchanged wrapped posies of spring flowers, comprising three, or five, or seven stems. Any other numbers were unlucky. Some children offered posies to us. I found a small container and plunged them into water, inviting the children into our modern kitchen, with its extended breakfast bar instead of a table.

They ate the cake I offered, but did not stay long. I stood in the playground watching their departure, thinking how appropriate it was to see actual children there.

Afterwards, the birds chattered, then swooped down to snatch my scattered crumbs in the school yard. They mobbed each other: sparrows, chaffinches and a large blackbird pecking in the grass. Would they nest in the eaves high against the roof, desperate to feed their young chicks?

In the centre of the eaves, on the outside, at the front of the schoolroom, stood a prominent statue of the virgin mother. I imagined they might nest there, in that niche.

A metal balustrade set in the stonework guarded her sculptured figure, clothed, as always, in colourful blue. She nestled, too. Had they freshly painted her at the time of the renewal of the roof? She gazed down in peace and, for a moment, I wondered how long the statue had stood there, witnessing it all.

I returned inside through a door in the *ballroom*, which I had opened earlier, to ventilate the area. Condensation had formed on the long drop of the wall of window glass. I sniffed the air, identifying the sugary sweetness of lily of the valley. The scent drifted lightly at first, but then powerful and cloying to the point of nausea. I looked for the source and noticed something in a corner. As I approached, I saw a huddled figure, and retreated, startled and on tiptoe, but she did not see me. Instead, the woman looked upwards along the wooden beams and then down again across the room. I followed her gaze. She was peeking through her fingers at Bernadette, who stood outside. I saw the figure more clearly now and realised what she was when she drew her veil across her face. Was she frightened of the little girl? Meanwhile, Bernadette slid her diminutive hands into the pockets of her pinafore and skipped across the tiles to the door. Not the arched classroom door – that's long gone, and I had seen the original plans – but that was where she disappeared. As she left, the nun crouched forward and rocked back and forth in a silent, troubled fashion. Then she knelt and took up a rigid attitude with her head bowed in prayer. I did not linger, but left again through the open door to the courtyard. By arrangement, I met the priest the following weekend; his relative youth surprised me, and he told me he was indeed a rarity, as France was a secular state, and few came forward with vocations except for dangerous ministries in far-off places. He stayed in the village overnight to take several services, as it was a day of obligation on that Sunday for those who still held to their faith. He had heard of my interest in the former inhabitants of the School House and the tragic event of a child's death at the hands of a parent.

"Parish records have an entry for Bernadette's birth," Father Robert said. "You are welcome to look at those. I keep them in the sacristy. And the marriage of her parents. There is also a scrapbook – a 'commonplace book' they called it in those days – which includes details of what happened when Bernadette's father was taken away, and what they said at the trial. You have been to the nearby town?"

"Yes, of course, but only for shopping … Should I find a library or other source…? We are not here in France for very long periods at a time. Not yet, anyway."

Father Robert assured me that the mayor could provide copies of written accounts by diverse people, both officialdom and popular hearsay. He would talk to the mayor on my behalf. When I asked if it was recorded how the nuns had reacted to the child's death, he studied me with a more serious expression.

"Much of the controversy you have already encountered in the village is about the nun called Sister Mercy."

Of course, it made me think of the strange figure I had recently seen; the nun in the schoolroom, but I said nothing of it. Would I seem too weird?

"What do you want to do with this material? Because they still talk of it here and it is a controversial story, even though it is long ago in a distant past," he said.

That much I had already gathered when talking to the villagers in the bar. It had bordered on quite a heated debate.

"If you lived in the old schoolhouse, wouldn't

you want to know something about those who came before?" I hoped that my question reassured him.

*****

It was late summer when we returned for the last time to complete the renovations. After that, we would use the schoolhouse as and when we pleased during the seasons. It would be possible to rent it out for periods, perhaps? Additional income could help with maintenance and heating. A family Christmas in France?

We had laid the patio and bought some attractive, if not wholly comfortable, metal garden furniture in a vast warehouse store of second-hand resalable goods in the nearest town. A curiosity of a place, in which I often drifted around fingering strange objects whose original purpose was unknown and fascinated by the detritus of a former age. But there were also useful bits and pieces of furniture. The staff would weigh the goods, and you could take them away by making a voluntary donation. When I asked why the weighing, they explained that for the statistics they had to show the entire enterprise was worthwhile and contributed to the town's targets. It was nothing to do with value, and everything to do with recycling.

I sat on one of the patio chairs, a cushion tucked under me, and a box of material on the wrought-iron table in front of me. Dozing and disinclined to make much effort, but the mayor had provided papers from the archives this time. I needed to see if anything would satisfy his further searches on my behalf.

I had picked up account books from the period when the school functioned, and knew from the newspaper accounts of the trial, and the scrapbook, or commonplace book, more of the events of that year. It was an uncomplicated, although tragic, story. Today, the father's momentary act that caused the accidental death of a child would not be punished with the death penalty, even if it existed. His remorse was dreadful and foreshadowed everything leading up to the trial.

At first, I did not realise what I held in my hand. A small bundle, tied with a thin black ribbon. The ink was still clear and the handwriting legible and plain. It was the writing of the period and, I knew, in France it would have been as universal for that time as the style taught in French schools is today. By the time I had finished reading it, I knew not only who the crouched figure in the schoolroom was, but also that I must show it to the priest.

It was the month of May when they took Bernadette's father away. We heard the growing roar of the villagers, who gathered to witness the cart carrying him several kilometres for judgement in the nearest town. We rushed to the windows in our dormitory; silent in our haste, knowing that our curiosity was unseemly, if not sinful, but unable to resist such a clamour from the outside world. Functional and forbidding was our convent dormitory, with its rows of iron framed beds. Between them, they had placed only a modesty screen to aid our private devotions. We peered through the metal grilles outside the dormitory windows on that May day. The cart paused outside. The Mayor strode down the steps from the town hall opposite our school. He silenced the crowd in an instant by his presence. I saw the prisoner, Bernadette's father, shackled in the cart. He raised his head and stared long and hard at the windows of our dormitory floor, and I drew back in alarm as he shook his fist. His mouth gaped wide, and he drew back his lips against his teeth as he shouted. The fury in his face!

I blanched and was faint. My Sisters' faces revealed their surprise and concern, and their arms offered support. They assisted me to my bed, but I would not sit down on it, because it was against the Rule at that time of the day.

It was not only the anger of Bernadette's father as he appeared that morning, but also the violence of the toothache. Together, they destroyed my composure. The pain had raged for so long. To admit it would be to show a weakness. I had debated the disclosure of it for weeks through my prayers.

Sister Joan had skills in the treatment of minor ailments. She had been discreet in giving me a small bottle of tincture against the toothache. I had applied it with increasing recklessness. I had told her it was effective. That was a lie, but with good intentions. She had smiled and whispered in the time honoured way, 'As the tooth is on the mend, offer up any remaining discomfort to our Lord.'

I had lied, and the pain seethed on into delirium.

It was the pain of my tooth that afternoon – a shattering spike in my temple, which had

*turned down my eye in the corner and made it weep – that caused the tragedy.
I had been so patient with Bernadette before. I knew she was slow and awkward with her needle and could not keep her tongue in her mouth when she struggled to form letters on her slate. But she knew her prayers and spoke them with eyes shut, her curling eyelashes close against her cheek, and never peeped through them in boredom and unbelief like so many other girls. That afternoon, I had lost my temper. I had lost restraint. I had let my heart fill with disdain for her backwardness. When I placed the dunce's cap on her head, she looked at me with such confusion. Then she lowered her eyes and throughout that afternoon she seemed to fix her gaze on one spot by her feet: a split or knot-hole in the floorboard. Her narrow shoulders on her tiny frame seemed to shrink as they drooped further and further in her humiliation.
Pure-hearted Bernadette had the virtue of truthfulness in abundance. When she returned home from school that day, she told her father of her punishment. Perhaps she was still confused, and hoped for enlightenment from her Papa.
Bernadette's father was a proud man though,*

and a frustrated one. Bernadette had only two sisters, and he wanted a son. His wife had struggled so in her confinements, and it was common gossip amongst her neighbours she was unlikely to bear another child, neither girl nor boy. When Bernadette confessed her punishment and told him of her long, silent afternoon standing in the corner wearing the dunce's cap, he hit her. Bernadette fell and split her head.
It is the passions that destroys us.
I grieved to cause the destruction and death of such innocence. I railed against my inability to check my own passions until I realised that my anger was akin to her father's. My rage was like his own blinding moment, when a restrained feeling released, all in a flash, caused a forever damning act.
That realisation was the end of hope. My hands tremble now as I look around the vacant, dusty schoolroom. I cannot control them. I hold them in front of me and look at them, but they do not seem to be a part of me, because calloused and red they look like hands which have known only blameless work.
Sister Superior finally took my private confession. I had begged her to do it with

such persistence. I could not let my desolation burden the thoughts of my Sisters in the public confession. How could I hold up my cruel, uncharitable act for their scrutiny, against their own meek remembrances of such minor infringements of the Rule of our convent? When they carried out the judgement on the wretched man, and Bernadette's siblings remained forever fatherless, the leaves in the playground were turning and beginning to fall from the horse-chestnut and the lime.
Of course, Sister Superior absolved me of all blame for Bernadette's death, for her father's actions and the judgement enacted upon him. She gave me penance only for my act of unkindness to Bernadette. She was gentle.
Advent is not a time of unalloyed joy and hope for the religious. The birth of Christ comes, but the weeks before are for rigorous self-examination. We contemplate the end of time in our world as much as the blessing of His grace. The snow came early that December and the cold was ferocious.
This is the hardest part to write. They found me in the wash house and cut me down in good time. Despair is a sin, too. So, I write this confession, already made to my Superior, and at her insistence because she demanded

it, though she would not read it, and it remains for a reminder that God is merciful, and I must keep it to remember our Lord's grace and not dwell on the sinfulness now. After I had read it, I felt a wave of compassion for this woman, whose conscience and way of life seemed tragic and out of time. I knew I would not show the confession to Nick until I had spoken with Father Robert.

*****

"I assume you are *not* thinking about exorcism, Carol?" said Father Robert. He gave me a half smile, but his frown made me realise I was treading on thin ice. We had become agreeable fellow researchers, but this would be a step too far.
"Not at all. I just wondered what you made of it. As a priest, of course I realise that it is controversial. But I would like to remove both 'presences' if I could, and this tale has further unnerved me."
"It's from a long time ago and has no relevance, you know," he said. "Let me have another look." We were in the kitchen, and he had accepted a cup of black coffee from the machine, and dropped a couple of brown

sugar lumps into it. I had bought macaroons from the village bakery; a favourite of his.

"I think the one 'presence' ties down the other in the schoolroom, and the courtyard too, which was the playground. And that idea works both ways. Do you think that is possible?" I asked.

The priest finished his coffee. I doubted he would offer an explanation. The church did not hold with superstition. But he was a young man and perhaps more open to the ideas of others. I thought of the Hamlet quote: 'There are more things in heaven and earth ....'

"There is a member of another congregation for whom I say Mass. She is involved in some marginal matters." The priest got up and tucked the bar stool under the breakfast worktop. "She isn't the traditional old wise woman either, nothing like that. I will speak to her."

He arranged a meeting after the following weekend's church services. I met Marguerite in the bar mid-week for an aperitif before the *plat du jour*. In her forties, perhaps, strong browned arms with rolled up sleeves and a mass of long wavy hair. She had been working in her mother's potager, weeding a vast bed of vegetables. Her French was quick and hard to follow, and she used patois vocabulary at times. This country dialect eluded me, but she was quick to replace it with French words when she saw my confusion.

Her explanation of the intertwined nature of the two – the child and the nun called Mercy, if it was she – resonated with me. She said that the two had never been reconciled to each other and remained therefore in a limbo in the schoolroom. Not ghosts exactly, she thought, more in terms of images from memory. 'Fleeting shades'. I was not the only person who had seen them, but my husband and I were the ones who had bought and refurbished the building and upset an equilibrium – *une position d'equilibre* – the translation was not difficult. Her solution was bizarre, but I was willing to try it with her. She knew where the graves were of the child and also of the nuns. Mercy's grave was a solitary unmarked one outside the main cemetery of the nuns who had lived and worked in the schoolroom. That was because she had attempted suicide.

The idea was to take a sample of earth from each grave, with the sort of tool that geologists might use, but on a much smaller scale. We needed to go deep. The events of almost two centuries and the subsequent impact on the burial grounds could be considerable. Then the cylindrical samples of earth would be exchanged from one grave to the other. This would reunite them physically, whatever shape or form the entities might take. Marguerite did not draw me into her interpretation, and the language barrier would not have permitted it. After this was done, she would ask Father Robert to say a prayer over both graves. That he had already assented to, regardless of what we were intending to do with the graves themselves.

It was not a misty, wet morning that we chose for this task, though it felt strange and almost like a desecration. Marguerite and I had removed a square of rough turf and made our extraction of earth from each mound – though these were flat with the subsidence of the years and identifiable only by a headstone for the child and a marked cross for the nun. We replaced the rough grass removed and, to all appearances, we had done nothing.

The next day, Father Robert prayed over both graves in our presence and I felt a sense of relief. We had disturbed them. He had blessed them in repose and peace.

It was not quite the end. That summer was very hot and the room on the first floor and at the end of the building, which had not been renovated, was to be tackled. But when we opened the door, hundreds of dead flies covered the floor at the edges of the walls and skirting. The room was closed up and sealed, like the others, once. The flies must have hatched out and had nothing to eat, being unable to escape. I learned later of the rumour that it was Mercy's cell and was where she had attempted to kill herself. They had used the entire floor as the teaching nuns' cells, which were large and well lit by their windows.

We closed up the house at the end of that summer and locked away all the gardening tools, and the old-fashioned petrol lawnmower, in the outbuildings. We had planted the traditional hydrangeas along the stretch of wall which faced the courtyard. A neighbour had promised to keep them watered.

When we returned earlier in the following year, the lime tree in the courtyard was in blossom and an old man, who had gained our permission, was delicately picking them. To make a tisane for all the villagers, he had told us. It seemed like a good sign, and it was. I saw nothing unexpected or unexplained in those few delightful weeks of modest sunshine, neither then nor since. I believe there had been a reconciliation.

INTO THE LIGHT

It was never a particular, regular day of the week when she came. Laura got out of the car and softly clicked shut the door before locking it. He hated it when she slammed the car door. He said that it was a woman's thing and a gender weakness.

She woke this morning with the usual shock of empty dread at yet another day and sat up, already tasting the blistering bile in her mouth. Laura washed her face and told the mirror that she had cried all her tears for today. It was not true, of course. The tears could well up at any unpredictable moment: the kindness of a stranger, an ill-considered allusion made by a friend in conversation, her sister's arm gripping her shoulder or, sometimes, the sound of his name.

Today, she came prompted by the same need. People said that she came here too often; it was an obsession, and it only increased her sadness, like the constant touching of an open wound. She thought only that we are all different, unique in our motives and the way we cope with the tangle of reason and emotion. It is why we fall in love with this man and not that one. It is a single, unmatched, unequalled individual.

When she arrived, her first self-imposed task was to read the words on the headstone. She read it over and over until, like the constant repetition of any single word or phrase, it became senseless, meaningless sounds in her head. It was not like that at first, but she had made it so.

Laura tidied the grave. People liked to let her know when they had visited the grave and left flowers. Sometimes they forewarned her of this act of remembrance. Unless the weather had been glacial, wet or windy, she could assess with surprising accuracy how long the flowers had been there because she had seen them in all their stages of decay.

It was so quiet. No sounds of the last of the season's grass cutting, no voices on the gravel paths down the steep slope, or the hum of distant traffic, and no planes cut through the sky above. Not even, at that moment, any birdsong.

He loved birds, knew all their names, their warbles and trills, their colours, the pattern of their flight. She learned some of them, too. At first she shouted at him, when he stamped on the brakes, drew to a sudden, dangerous halt on an undulating country lane, just because he had glimpsed the glittering, iridescent feathers of a kingfisher on the river. Then her own enthusiasm overcame her fears over the years. She knelt to remove the fall of autumnal leaves. She did not kneel to pray; he was the one who had retraced his religion in the last months, reviewed it, and revived it. The reason why it was a burial and not a cremation. In her lack of belief, she could not hold on to a reunion in the hereafter. There were only these days, these visits, and she did not want to dwell on what she knew had happened to his physical presence, sealed away from the air, but not inviolate. His religion said that you must not despair.

The leaves she raked up with her bare hands varied: a pallid green, yellow, or blotted with red, or had turned a wrinkled, crisp brown. She preferred the winter and the bleak, bare shapes of the stripped trees outlined against lowering skies to the desiccated fall of dead leaves. At least in winter, the dying had finished.

Laura stood and brushed at the mud on the knees of her outworn brown trousers. Rain spattered them, adding to her unkempt appearance. She had always loved clothes, fabrics, and fashion. The idea came to her that perhaps the Victorians had got it right about mourning that the widow's weeds were not just an outward show. Shrouded in lustreless black for a year and a day, they progressed, under the social conventions, to a less momentous change to grey, then to shades of lavender and lilac.

She imagined what the preparations would involve. First, the measuring of her leaner, pining body amidst the heady sight of the new, softer, lighter, gentler fabrics with their silken sheen. An unravelled bolt held up to the window to see the full glory of its colour. The fittings for the dress and the sensation of silk draped against her skin, while she glanced in the mirror at the new, unrecognised reflection. When she, as a woman of those times, pulled the gown down over her hidden, frilled petticoats, did a transformation run through the body and deep into the veins, like a charge of new-fashioned electricity, or even a charge of life?

Perhaps it was not just rules of social etiquette governing your outward appearance, but a moral imperative; grieving had its limits. There were layers and you had to subsume them, one by one. You had to come up into the light.

She had thought it would be less painful once an entire year had passed, enduring and living through all the anniversaries: his birthday, her birthday, Christmas, their Wedding Anniversary, the day they met and the day he proposed marriage. On that day, he had knelt amongst all their friends, encouraged by a few glasses of wine, moved by his own emotions, which were so shy. With that memory, she had to pause now and took a deep breath.

He was hopelessly unromantic and never remembered special dates. She had bombarded him with heart-shaped stones found on the beach, handmade cards, pathetic poetry and embarrassing notes tumbling out from where she had hidden them in his office. His face showed his horror if she tried to take his hand in public or kiss him on the cheek.

It was not easier with these reminiscences. She clung to her grief as something tangible: to diminish it would be to diminish him.

Laura picked up the rain-filled water jar and wedged it down behind the headstone. She filled a plastic bag with the heaped, crushed leaves ready for disposal, but stopped and tilted her head. *Is that a bird? So close?* She listened harder. *It's a whistling, fluting sound. I know that bird's song.* She dug deep into her memories.

They went on a camping holiday to the Auvergne in France. Arriving late one evening in May, with rain streaming like a torrent down the windscreen. She cowered on entering the tent, which was already in place on the camp-site, with a bottle of wine and some flowers placed on the little fold-up table inside. They trailed mud, and she flinched, thinking in desperation that she would never keep it clean.

He told her that cleanliness was not the point of camping. He accompanied her in the middle of the night to the toilet block and afterwards, tucking her in against his body in the tent's shelter, soothed her with soft words until she slept.

When they awoke, the tent was sun-filled. Their nearest neighbours sat outside drinking coffee and brandy with their breakfast, smiling as they gazed up at an almost cloudless, blue sky. The couple explained they came every year in May in order to avoid the crowds and the school holidays.

Laura remembered standing in the doorway on that first camping morning. She pulled back and pinioned the tent flap and watched the poplar trees swaying in a light breeze, listened to the river a few yards away and the piercing cries of the campsite's peacocks. After that, she tried in vain to get the peacocks to display for her husband's camera. *How he loved photography.* Outrageous and superior in their arrogant sashaying, wilful and adamant not to satisfy the desire of onlookers to admire the colours of their wonderful patterned feathers, the peacocks had ensured he could not capture a satisfactory image for the long, dark winter evenings to follow their holiday.

He rose earlier than her. Usually, he left her sleeping, but on that morning near the end of their holiday, he crept back into the tent after dawn, and whispered with excited urgency. She followed him on tiptoe down to the river bank, sleepy, but listening as bid. It was the first time she heard a Golden Oriole, but they never saw it. Not once did they manage even a glimpse of the secretive bird.

Only a few moments had passed in that reverie. She slipped back into the present and listened hard again, then crept towards the line of trees bordering the graveyard. The continuous song grew louder. She peered

upwards to the highest point in the canopy of the trees where the birds preferred to perch.
A movement of undulating flight and a splash of bright yellow made her rigid and wait, holding her breath, to see the male bird. He flew into full sight and her mouth gaped open in amazement and sheer delight. She recognised him by the black wings and the distinctive yellow body of a blackbird's size. It gloried in a sun yellow – the same colour produced by the organic pigment in the yellowing of those autumn leaves which she had, a few minutes before, so despised in their withered fall.
She stood and watched, but the bird did not appear again. Laura returned to the grave and bent to pick up the plastic bag of leaves and other detritus. How she wished she could have shared that moment with him. How boyishly excited he would have been. She remembered the look on his face with his eyes lit up and his mouth beaming, while she imagined him jumping for joy.
It led to her remembrance of all the photographs. An untidy clutter of jumbled prints of all sizes, stacked in a large, old cardboard box with torn flaps. Although she had pledged so many times to do it, she was

still loath to go through them. They needed putting in order, selecting and discarding, mounting in the albums which she had bought and given to him as presents. The earliest years of married life.
In later years, protesting, he accepted a digital camera. After that, he downloaded his 'snaps' and enhanced them, forgetting that he had once argued it was akin to cheating. Instead, he discovered all the new possibilities, magnifying and realising the perfect stills of images he had held in his head and which a hand less steady could no longer seize.
The earlier photographs of their courtship, when they had first set up a home together, showed them looking into the camera with all the positive assurance of youth. Were those not the most essential of their relationship? The undiluted essence of their love? It was obvious from those deep gazes that they would stay together until death did them part.

As she got up and stood to mouth her farewell at the headstone, she made him a promise, which this time she would keep. *I will go home and sort through the photographs.*
It would be a step to show that she was coping, and an outward show to others, that

she could look again upon those photographs of an intimate portrayal of a life together, and put them in order as a history of their past. In the innermost part of her, lay the real significance of this project. She could come up, stumbling, into the light.

FLASH FICTION INTRO

Short and even shorter stories written to a challenging limit on the number of words, or the time allowed. Sometimes both! As in sudden impromptu prompts to write to in a creative writing group session. The clue is often in the title.

The stories are in different formats; including mainly dialogue, or a letter, as well as short scenes. Even a story in the shape of a literary vignette.
All have to comply with the idea of a story and have a beginning, middle and an end!

A STAB IN THE DARK

Susannah was totally outside her comfort zone in this environment. Even 'comfort zone' was an expression she had only learned that morning in the discussion session at the retreat in which she hoped to unwind.

It was her husband's idea to 'gift' her this course as a birthday present. An important birthday, of course; one of the decade's variety. That summer they had already enjoyed two weeks abroad in an exotic resort, but this was something just for her.

'Me' time they call it, don't they? You deserve it!' he had said. He knew how much she loved learning.

At first, Susannah had been very excited at the prospect. Although they had some interests in common (how did couples survive without that?), even their sumptuous holiday in July had involved more food and wine and lazing in the sunshine than was really to her taste. Not that she was at all adventurous. Not like their friendly next-door neighbours who had gone white-water rafting the previous year. 'At their age!' She had commented, and of course, her husband, John, agreed.

'Asking for trouble,' John said. 'It's all about an 'Adrenalin rush'. Some people get addicted to that and do all kinds of daft things.'

When the neighbours, Roger and Joan, returned home, with the severe after effects of a water-born bug, they had both felt vindicated and superior. Although they had been assiduous in offers of help. They had devoted many hours listening, over pots of herbal tea, to the story of the prevalence of the disease, with a list of abhorrent symptoms and the nauseating consequences of contracting it.

Susannah had cleaned, shopped and visited the doctors' surgery on the other side of town to pick up medication. Glad to be of use. But the tea with which she received recompense and the endless health prognostications had been tedious. Her husband, John, avoided most of that. Susannah felt relieved to go away on her own for an indulgent week.

On the evening of her arrival, after a delicious meal, Susannah phoned her husband. Sitting by her bed in a luxurious room, with a wonderful view of the 18th century parkland, she felt pampered. She slept well and awoke refreshed and eager to begin. That call had gone well, but doubts soon crept in. The following morning's discussion of their schedule alarmed her. Why had John picked *this* course for her treat? She knew nothing of oriental religions and even less of martial arts.

The bruising gained in the session on the mats during the afternoon still smarted hours later. She had no wish to kick the woman in front of her. Such a kind face! Susannah stirred with guilt again at the mere thought of it. But the woman had been pleasant about the impact of the blow inflicted on her, even complimentary. 'Nice one!' was the expression she had used before returning the assault with good measure. Looking around at the assortment of women present, through an eye which was closing, Susannah had squinted at their facial expressions. All of them looked tense, determined, and aggressive. Were these women actually *enjoying this*? Susannah wondered.

Curled on her bed later that day, and rubbing her sore back, Susannah picked up her mobile to confront John and demand why she should remain in the centre, even if it was so beautifully situated and offered, in theory, so much comfort.

'Where on earth did you find this course, John? And, more to the point, why in God's name *this* course?

'Aren't you enjoying it anymore?' he asked. He sounded hurt and surprised.

'Did you get a brochure and read it?'

'Well, yes. But I didn't read it through. I wouldn't understand all that stuff, anyway.'

'What do you mean – that stuff?'

John's response was hesitant. She could tell from his tone that he was confused. Was an apology forming?

'I'm not sure, but from what you texted to our eldest daughter earlier on today – and I have had an earful from her – I realise now that I didn't understand properly. What it entailed. It was a stab in the dark, and last minute. In the heat of the moment, while looking at that lovely photo of the place. It looked so peaceful. You know Roger and Joan thought you needed a relaxing break.'

Possibly, John was consulting the brochure at that moment. Susannah could hear glossy pages turning. She waited, her mind racing.

'So that is what ... *Chinese Taoist Contrapuncture ...Thought and Physicality* involves. I'm sorry, love. I thought it was ... philosophy!'

BIRD TALK

"I'll turn off the birdsong CD. It's teeming down and I hope he gets wet. Try again, Mimi. I say 'Hello, Roger'. You say, 'Goodbye and good riddance'. Come on, you *crazy* bird."

Cray-zee! Cray-zee!

"No, Mimi. You were word *perfect* yesterday. I say "Hello Roger" and you ….

Hello, purr-fect.

"Here's a nut. Don't nip my fingers; it hurts! Lovely feathers. Aren't you a pretty girl? OK, take a rest then and tuck you head under, my poor little darling."

Hello Roger, darrr-ling.

"You're getting worse. Who taught you to roll your 'r's, anyway? Another nut, Mimi? That's a good girl. Don't talk with your mouth full."

Pretty. Pretty. Hello, Roger.

"That's the bell! At least this will be over soon and I won't see him again. Neither will you, Mimi, and he never liked you much."

Hello, Roger! Hello, Roger! That *cheetin* bastard.

"Oh God! Where did you hear that? Was it with my friends ... on the phone? Mimi, I'm going to have to put this cloth over your cage now, so you don't talk."

*****

"I put all your books in this box, Roger. Make it quick; I'm on my way out."

"Still got that mangy bird, then?"

"Don't do that, Roger! Leave the cover on Mimi, please. Just leave her alone."

Hello Roger. That *cheetin* bastard.

"Flipping hell, Lucy. Why did you teach her that? I'm off."

"In that case, goodbye and good riddance. Thank you Mimi."   **DOOR SLAMS**

I COULD HAVE LAUGHED....

Friday the thirteenth. Everyone knows to be wary of that. Yet I could not avoid it. Not the day itself. I took extra care driving along the narrow country lanes because I had deliberately left only a small time frame, and it was closing in on me. The lowering sky reflected my mood as the trees dripped a cascade of rain like a plastic waterfall, which rolled down my windscreen so that I had to flip the wipers onto 'fast'.
I arrived, climbed the winding stairs as directed, and almost at once took my seat. No time lost here in this, to my nostrils, atmosphere of less than anodyne smells.
"There was an Englishman, an Irish man and a Scot..." The muffled words came through as I felt the initial perspiration trickling down my neck. I gripped the arms of the chair and waited; anticipating the moment, clenching my fists.
It passed into something else; a complete reversal of that dread. The expected jolt of

unrelenting fear did not happen. My muscles relaxed in a sudden flush, sweeping downwards from my face and neck. It was akin to joy.

Afterwards – not long in retrospect – with unrestrained relief, I spoke.
"I could have laughed, but I thought I might choke! All those things in my mouth. Your jokes are far better than any soft, lulling music."
The dentist smiled.

KARMA CHAMELEON

"You're so difficult today; you keep changing." He flipped the tip of the hair brush and smeared it along the edge of the Prussian blue on his artist's palette.

"What do you mean? Changing? That's normal. I express what I feel."

"To a degree," he acknowledged. "Of course, the colour changes with your emotions. But I want to get the essence of you, and I am known to be skillful. Your present blue is cold and distant. Think of the good times we have had and change it, please."

She swept the fin of her tail forward in an enticing curve and tilted her head back beneath the shadowed brim of her hat.

"That's better! A warm peach," he said.

She heard the stool creak as he settled again upon it. His contentment did not last. The even breathing turned into a rasp as she changed once more. He peered over the frame of the easel. "Not grey! What are you thinking? You'll ruin it..."

"I feel distant, lost." You have replaced me in your affections. That new model, the one with the glassy eyes and sharp-edged scales."

His palette clattered to the ground, and he slithered towards her and rose up menacingly in front of her. "She is nothing to me. I needed a new muse, that's all." Bending towards her, he touched a sensitive claw to the mottled flap beneath her mouth, then caught some moisture trickling from her eye. She could tell he believed she forgave him as she adjusted her hat and leaned forward over him.

The blood curdled thickly from his abdomen when she extracted the skewer of the hat pin. His body thwacked down onto the floor.

"Why are you staring at me?" she said to his dulled eyes, as she saw the angry scarlet hue of her own head reflected in them.

TELL THE BEES

"He thinks I won't go through with this!" Sarah said aloud. She braced herself, with hands on hips, and kicked a tuft of grass. Looking up at the incongruous blue sky and the slow drift of clouds, she had to admit it was another ironically beautiful day. The bees hummed.
"I want some honey!" Susie came bounding across the lawn, skipping and leaping. Sarah swept her up and hugged her close. "Not today, precious. Maybe tomorrow."
The phone rang and Sarah stumbled into her house, planting her daughter on a chair in front of her breakfast.

Of course, it will be Richard. I don't want to talk about it. I've filed for divorce.
  "Please, Sarah. Please speak to her." Richard's voice was breaking. "I didn't want to tell you until I knew for certain. She's my sister! It's taken me so long to trace her … and then we couldn't wait to meet up. You've no idea!"

There was a long pause. Had he cut her off?

"How could you believe that gossip from your friends? Why couldn't you trust me?" He sounded angry now.
Sarah looked at Susie finishing her breakfast. Blinking to make sure it wasn't a dream, and promised to call him back. She took Susie's hand and led her into the garden. As they approached the beehive, Susie whooped with joy and excitement.
 "Shh, sweetie."

It can wait. I'll tell the bees tomorrow. She smiled, and in the sudden sensation, brushed her fingertips along the taunt skin of her cheeks, tracing a tear.

THE DROP

She sucked in a deep, nervous breath as she sat down on the park bench and tried hard to relax. The backdrop of a patchy blue sky neither matched her mood nor contributed any warmth. Sunshine would help. So much to think about.

Her stomach tautened at the sudden glimpse of the hands of her fellow sitter. They repulsed her; the scaled and mottled flesh of advanced age. She had not expected it, and realised the sight drew on some vague memory which induced her present disgust.

What if I fail? She thought.

Then she could smell him. The slight whiff of mildewed clothes and the fresher tang of...? The latter, at least, was not unpleasant.

Smoothing her skirt, she looked at him again, focussed on the springy curls of incongruous *black* hair on his chest. They peeped through above his unbuttoned frayed shirt. She adjusted her position, sat back against the wooden slats of the bench, and appeared to settle.

The man wheezed, coughed and spat; a globule of opaque liquid landed near her foot.

Katherine seized the moment. She slid her left foot out of the flimsy red sandal and massaged her toes. Repeating the action with her right foot, she twisted a sliver of folded paper from the heel of the sandal into her palm. Changing posture, leaning forward, and inching herself closer to the man, she spoke. *"My feet are killing me,"* she said, and waited.

"OK. Stop!" called Robert. The audience of three burst into spontaneous applause. Katherine and her companion stood up and bowed mockingly towards them. She felt so much relief that she kept grinning as she stepped down.

"Did *anyone* see the drop?" Robert asked. He leapt up from the pit between the front row and the platform.

A crescendo of negatives followed his question. Robert shook Katherine's hand. "Well done! We will make a spy of you, yet."

Braced by her achievement, Katherine turned to the young man beside her. "You need to button up your shirt. Dead giveaway. I could smell the greasepaint, too."

A ZOO INMATE ADDRESSES HIS VISITORS
Ambivalent about zoos, despite the conservation aspects, I always read the notices and one particular request inspired me.

Dear Predators

At first, I trembled and scurried away at the sight of you with your enormous presence and the looming shadows you cast. Sometimes you rap on the glass, and the sharp sound ricochets around my home. I knew it was not only your eyes that made me tremble. Those eyes which are so unlike my own; fixed and piercing, so that you must sway and turn to peer at me. Your heads and bodies have a strange rotation, too.

Once, I severed my tail in my distress at your tapping of the glass. It is a strenuous process to regrow a tail, and I will not forget it.

In the beginning, I did not know how I arrived in this place. I do not think I was born here, and I never knew my mother. When the others came and we made friends, I learned more. We conquered our instincts because there was plenty of food and nothing to contest. We have a lore amongst us now, and we piece together those patchy lost elements of our lives.

When you creatures – held back beyond our cages, contained, or removed from us altogether – no longer threaten, we raise the coloured flap on our throats and talk to each other inside our glass cage. You can see that my home is small, but as we commune with each other, we dream of great distances. We picture darting into a multitude of different crevices and sitting in deep contentment on a series of rocks.

The warmth enlivens me as I raise my head to the glass and to the light. I hope to wander and bask in the sun. Some new friends talk of the heat generated on the rocks and stones at mid-day under an open sky, and of a breeze – a waft of warm air which moves over heads and bodies. Here, all is still, and the light is not from the sun.

The raucous sound that comes from your mouths as you lean forward enervates us. We retreat and hide from you. At noon, we see you place food in your mouth, so that the noise stops. You eat laboriously, folding the food with tongues which appear short and unskilled: unable to flick and catch your prey. We do not recognise what you eat, but we have seen you try to catch flies and other insects. You wave your legs ineffectually at them because you always fail.

If you could reach us, released from your own containment, kept at bay by the glass, then you would eat us: roast our bodies using a heat greater even than the rays of the sun. They say you once called us edible 'fish of the desert', so we have reason to fear. There is a story told many times over, at night when all is quiet and the flow of our blood slows towards the oblivion of sleep that the glass of our cage shattered once! Although it immobilised most of my brothers in their confusion at the noise, as a blast of air stirred the loose ground beneath their legs and feet, one of us ventured out towards the light.

He did not escape for long, but at least they did not eat him. They gathered him up and returned him to his home. Then he told us of the initial shock to his senses, turning into an ecstasy because he had never felt as alive as outside the cage. After he told the tale, he did not linger long in his body because he pined for those momentary sensations. Yet his story lives on.

I often dream of escape from the glass, but *you* lie beyond it. I am denied the sun which you enjoy, though the glass fulfils a purpose. It keeps *you* – our predators – at a distance from us. The ever lengthening passing of time also makes us feel more secure from you.

I have a simple request. Please, do not tap the glass.

Yours in confinement,

A lizard

About Mary D Curd

AKA   M D Curd

I write novels, novellas and short stories. Writing has been important to me in one form or another for most of my life. So far I have published 3 novels in e and paperback format as part of a Victorian trilogy, and two novels in a new Historical mysteries series. The latter includes a split-time novel between the contemporary period and the 12th century, and another partly set in the 1920's.

Although I was born and lived most of my adult life on the SE coast of England, I have also lived in France for 12 years, and drew on that period for the next book; a novel set in a French Chateau, which moves between the contemporary period and the 1920s. We settled back in the UK in 2014 and love it here in Cornwall.

Settings are very important in my stories and I love to research historical periods and different cultures.

My husband is a great supporter of my writing. I have also been pleased to have short stories accepted in competitions and in anthologies. The latter for two local Writing Groups. It's a great way to find readers who give encouragement for what you are writing and hoping to complete! Input from readers is so important to me and I welcome reviews from anyone who has the time and the will.

https://www.amazon.co.uk/Mary-D-Curd/e/B07CNSJ4ZC%3Fref=dbs_a_mng_rwt_scns_

Printed in Great Britain
by Amazon